D1429261

SOMETHING VERY FISHY

SOMETHING VERY FISHY

by

NIGEL TRANTER

COLLINS
LONDON AND GLASGOW

First printed 1962

PRINTED AND MADE IN GREAT BRITAIN BY
WILLIAM COLLINS SONS AND CO. LTD.
LONDON AND GLASGOW

CONTENTS

CHAP.		PAGE
1.	Man in the Dark	11
2.	Doubting Samaritans	27
3.	The Wrecked Car	38
4.	Something A-missing	56
5.	Two-and-Two Make . . . ?	69
6.	To Tell or Not to Tell	79
7.	Bird Flown	95
8.	A Quick Decision	103
9.	Telling the Police	111
10.	Action!	120
11.	Solo Performance	126
12.	The Hunt is On	140
13.	Fugitive in the Heather	151
14.	Hide and Seek	167
15.	Mickey Pat's Farewell	183
16.	Postman's Knock	189

ILLUSTRATIONS

. . . . a youngish man with a great mop of red hair. — *page* 28

Mickey Pat had now backed out of the car. — 71

"You!" he jerked, grabbing the boy's arm. — 136

Ian was already crouching down. — 177

To H.

CHAPTER ONE

MAN IN THE DARK

"LET'S go and explore that old tower—Houndswyre Tower," Ian MacDonald proposed. "It looks mighty romantic, standing there on its rock. We've plenty of time."

His brother Don shook his curly head. "What's the use?" he demanded. "It's just another old Border peel. We've seen umpteen of them. All the same. Just a lot of mouldering old stones piled on top of each other—that's all."

"It's nothing of the sort, Don!" Ian protested. "It's an exciting place. Lots of thrilling things have happened there—fights and raids and reiving and tortures. You know that perfectly well." He quoted:

"Houndswyre Tower, well may ye glower,
O'er bonny Teviotdale,
For the blood you've spilled and the ill you've willed,
And the widows you've left to wail."

"Goodness—poetry now!" Don snorted. "What next?"

"It's not poetry! At least, it's not sissy poetry. It's a ballad. Border minstrelsy. Tough stuff. Look—I said I'd come with you to see the new dam they are building up at Brackenhope. *I* think dams and all that sort of thing are a bore. The least you can do is to come with me to look at Houndswyre Tower."

"All right, all right," Don grinned. "No accounting for tastes. Anything for peace and a quiet life! Let's go rubber-necking at old stones, and spouting poetry."

"Better than staring at bull-dozers, and moaning about pre-stressed concrete and metal fatigue!"

It was always this way with the two brothers, the best of friends though they were. Twins, and very like each other in build and feature, with their freckled faces, snub-noses and curly hair, they were nevertheless as different as chalk from cheese. The blue-eyed, quick-witted, and quick-tempered Don was the leader, eager, swift to act, interested in the future, in constructing things, planning to be a civil engineer; Ian, brown-eyed and more thoughtful, was quieter, more fond of books—but no softy. Certain deer poachers up in the Cairngorm Mountains had had plenty of proof of that, not so long before.

The boys wheeled their bicycles off the road and hid them behind a hedge. Then they slanted down across the grassy sheep-dotted hillside, to cross the little valley between them and the rocky crag from which thrust the proud, red-brown tower of Houndswyre. All about them the green, rounded hills of the

Borderland stretched in an endless pattern of ridge and range and rampart. They were gentler-seeming hills than the rugged Highland mountains that the boys loved so well—but with something challenging about them, too. Don and Ian had arrived in Teviotdale only the day before, for a ten-day Easter holiday with their aunt, at Denholm-on-the-Green, wondering rather how they were going to fill in their time; their Aunt Mary, though very nice, was elderly, unmarried, and not a riot of excitement. They need not have worried.

Leaping across the burn in the floor of the valley, where lambs frisked and scampered, they climbed up the steep, rock-strewn slope beyond, where the yellow gorse already crackled in the spring sunshine. On the very crest of the ridge the peel-tower rose, stern and defiant, as though growing out of the rock. It was tall and square, reaching up four stories to a crumbling parapet, with a garret story still higher within the broken, stone-slated roof. Its walls were built of the local stone, rough-hewn and massive. But despite its fierce air of dominating all the rolling countryside around, Houndswyre Tower was not very large; only about thirty feet square, in fact, with a single room on each floor, and a winding turnpike stair coiling up within the thickness of the walling at one corner. The windows were tiny, barred with rusty iron yetts or grilles, and wide, splayed gunloops like open mouths guarded the single-arched doorway.

That doorway had not held a door for a hundred years.

Panting with their climb, the brothers stared upwards. Some jackdaws flew out from the broken battlements.

"Not much of a place!" Don declared. "No size at all, really. You wouldn't think that it would be responsible for much spilled blood, ill-will, and widows' wails!"

"You shouldn't judge by mere size," Ian said. "Old castles aren't quite the same as your dams and bridges, that you measure by cubic capacity and maximum load!"

"Come on, then. Let's go in and get it over with."

Stepping in over the hollowed stone threshold—which, Ian pointed out, undoubtedly had been worn down by generations of mailed feet, and which his brother said much more like hob-nailed boots—they felt the dank chill of the place strike them like a blow. It was extraordinary how much colder it was in that stone-vaulted, ground-floor chamber than in the sunny April day outside. And silent. Without realising it, the boys' voices dropped to a whisper. They took one look inside the dark empty vault, lit only by an arrow-slit at one end and a gunloop at the other, and then turned to the worn and broken stairway nearby, to climb to higher, and, it was to be hoped, brighter floors above.

They were almost at first-floor level, Don leading, when Ian stopped.

"Did . . . did you hear something, Don?" he asked.

"No? Did you? Hear what?"

"I . . . I don't quite know. I'm not sure. It sounded . . . rather like a groan!"

"A groan? Don't be daft, Ian! That's the worst of an imagination like yours. It would be one of these crows or jackdaws or whatever they . . ."

Don's scornful words faded away, as he turned to stare at his brother. Distinctly, from somewhere within those echoing bare stone walls, sounded a strange moaning noise.

Wide-eyed the two boys looked at each other. It was not a nice sort of sound, at all.

Ian swallowed. "You heard it . . . ?"

"Yes. I wonder . . . ?" They were speaking now in very quiet whispers indeed. "Where did it come from? Up or down?"

"I don't know. It just seemed to come out of the walls."

They waited for a few moments, ears stretched. Apart from a faint drip-drip somewhere, there was a heavy silence.

"That's impossible," Don said at length. "Coming out of the walls, I mean. You'll be telling me the place is haunted, next."

Ian swallowed. "Widows' wails . . . !" he began, a little unsteadily.

"Widows' grandmothers! More likely the wind, moaning down some old chimney."

"But there isn't any wind to-day."

"Well—there may have been an odd gust, just then. This is a high-standing place that might catch a wind. Come on—let's get up on to the battlements."

"I . . . I don't know if we should, Don."

"Look—it was you who wanted to explore this dump, wasn't it? Spouting all that stuff about glowering tower and spilled blood . . ."

Once again Don stopped in mid-sentence. It was not exactly a moan this time. More of a whimpering murmur, ending in muttered words. Quite clearly words were spoken—though what they were could not be made out.

"Goodness—that came from down there! Below." Ian gasped.

"But we've been there. We looked into that stone-arched place. It was quite empty."

"Yes, I know. But . . . you heard it. What should we do?"

"We'd better go down again, anyway."

Tiptoeing now, they turned back down the stairs.

At the foot, the open doorway drew them towards the sunshine like a magnet. They took one quick look into the vault, assured themselves that it was indeed empty, and were heading out over the threshold without further delay when, from quite close at hand somewhere, a mumbling voice spoke.

"Och, by all the saints . . . ! Mercy on us—let me out o' here. By the powers, it's dying I am, here. It's me leg, me leg . . ."

"Hang it all—that's no ghost!" Don cried, in sudden relief. "At least, if it is, it sounds mighty like an Irish one, to me!"

"Someone in trouble," Ian said. "Sounds as though he was trapped, somewhere. But where?"

They went back inside, peering around them.

"It had a sort of hollow sound. Must be in the wall, somewhere. You were maybe right enough, Ian."

"Perhaps if we call out, he'll answer us? Guide us."

"Where are you?" they shouted, together. "Can we help?"

Only the echo of their own voices answered them.

"This is mighty queer . . ." Don began, when his brother interrupted.

"Look—here's a place. In this dark corner behind the stair. A doorway. And steps, leading down."

They stared in and downward. It was pitch dark down beyond a narrow entrance in the walling. They could not see how many steps there were, and where they led. But as the boys paused uncertainly, they heard a distinct stirring from somewhere below. Heavy breathing.

Doubtfully, the twins looked at each other.

"Why doesn't he answer?" Ian whispered softly.

"Goodness knows. Maybe it's just a tramp or something. Drunk, perhaps."

"He said he was dying, before. Could he have fallen down there and hurt himself? We don't know how far down it goes."

"Doesn't sound very far down. We can hear him quite plainly. Breathing." Don raised his voice. "I say—are you all right, down there? Can we help you?"

There was no reply.

"He must be unconscious, now. Maybe he was delirious before. If only we had a light."

"Well, we haven't," Don said. "We . . . we'd better just go down and have a look."

"But . . . should we? I mean . . ."

"We can't just go away now, and leave him there. Can we? It may be somebody in real trouble. If it's only a drunk, we can leave him there easily enough. But it's a funny place for a drunk to be. Come on."

Side by side, and so blocking the narrow stairway and preventing any pale indirect light from filtering down, they went slowly, one step at a time, feeling their way with the toes of their shoes—and, if the truth must be known, both ready to bolt back up again at a moment's notice.

Actually there were only five steps. Then they seemed to be standing on a damp, earthen floor. Obviously this was some sort of underground pit, dug into the rock of the ridge—probably the prison of the tower. Though they could not see walls or roof, or indeed anything at all, they could feel, somehow, that they were in a small, narrow place. It felt like a cave.

Somebody was taking long breaths, unevenly, only a yard or two away from them—half right.

With one accord the boys edged away, half left.

"Y-you there," Don's voice came suddenly, unsteadily. "Is anything wrong? Can we help you?"

Perfectly clearly, naturally, almost heartily, they were answered, in a rich Irish brogue. "Och and indeed you can, lads. Leastways, maybe you can. See —is it just the two o' you boys that's in it?"

Shaken now by the abrupt change in the situation, the twins hesitated. Ian indeed stepped back a pace, and found himself up against a dripping wall.

"There's just the two o' you, eh?" the voice repeated, a shade anxiously. Evidently the speaker could see better than his visitors.

"Yes," Don said. "Me and my brother. What . . . what are you doing in here? What's wrong?"

"Och, there's plenty wrong, boy. It's me ankle. And me ribs. Och, and me head, too. But sure, it's the ankle's the worst. It's hurted bad if it's not broke. I can't walk."

"I'm sorry," Don exclaimed. "But . . . how did it happen? How did you get in here? You couldn't have done all that by falling down these few steps."

"No," the man said. That was all.

Their eyes were getting more accustomed to the gloom now, and the boys began to be aware of a dark figure seemingly sitting propped up against a wall opposite, only a few feet away.

"What can we do to help you?" Ian asked. "Are you in great pain?"

"Sure, I'm in pain. Wicked pain. But—you wouldn't have a bite o' food on you now, would you, boys? Or a drink?"

"We've only got half a slab of chocolate left. You're hungry?"

"Not a bite or a drink's crossed my lips these twenty-four hours," they were told. "A-a-ah! Merciful saints—me leg!"

"Do you want this chocolate, then? It's all we have."

"Give it here, boy. Sure."

Ian moved over, the chocolate in his hand held out vaguely in the right direction. It was snatched from him far from vaguely, and they could hear that it was thrust into the man's mouth whole and almost before the silver paper was off. There seemed to be no doubt about the stranger's hunger at any rate.

"Look," Don said. "This is a terrible place for you to be in—however you got here. Can we get you out of this ghastly hole?"

"No, you can't. Never a bit o' it," the sufferer declared very determinedly, through the chocolate.

"But, why?"

"Wasn't I just telling you—I can't move at all."

"But if we helped you?" Ian urged him. "You say it's your leg. If it's only one leg, one ankle, then you could lean on us and hop. We'd at least get you out of this horrible pit."

"No, boy!" the other barked. "I'm fine here."

"Well," Don said. "If you're injured and in great pain, and you can't be moved, there's only one thing we can do—and that's go and get a doctor. To come to you here."

"You'll do no such thing! I'm having no doctors coming here," the man told them, almost angrily.

The brothers looked at each other in the darkness.

"I don't see that there's anything that we *can* do, in that case," Don declared. "But it seems jolly queer to me, I must say."

"Sure there's something you can do for me. If you're decent good boys. Fetch me some food and something to drink, see. And cold water and bandages to tie up my ankle. I've sprained it bad. Cold pads will be putting it right. Och, do that for me, lads, and I'll be outa here in two-three days, right as rain."

"Two or three days . . . !" Ian echoed. "In this hole?"

"I'm all right here, I tell you—if you'll fetch me a bite to eat and drink. And the water. And maybe some aspirins to kind o' lift the pain, see. And mind, boys—not a word to a living soul. I'll see it's worth your while."

Don drew a long breath. "It's . . . it's pretty obvious that you're in some sort of trouble," he said. "I mean, more than just your injuries. You've been, well, doing something you shouldn't—haven't you? And you can hardly expect us to help . . ."

"Och, I've done no one a mite o' harm, at all," the Irishman protested. "I call the dear saints above to witness. It's just meself liking a bit o' sport now and again, same as other folk. And a bite o' salmon's tasty."

"Salmon! Sport! You've been poaching, you mean?"

"Mercy on us—it's poaching is it when a poor man fancies a small bit of a fish out o' the river? And good sport when it's a rich man that does it? Sink me—that's the sort o' world it is!"

"Was it when you were poaching you had your accident?" Ian asked.

"Accident my foot! It was keepers did this to me—keepers and bailiffs, rot them! They beat me up. Just about half-killed me. They got the fish and did this to me—but I got away from them. I got away, and hid meself. In some bushes. Then I dragged meself here. Last night. In the dark. I saw this place against the sky, see. It was a bad business getting here, I tell you. But I reckoned I'd be safe here."

"Goodness!" Ian cried. "They hurt you like this? All for poaching a salmon?"

"They did, sink them! Four o' them, there were.

Big characters. What chance had I against the four? They got the fish and my gear, and they near killed me."

"The brutes!" Don exclaimed. "You should go to the police about this. These men—the keepers—have no right to set about you like this, I'm sure. They could have taken the fish, but . . ."

"It was a rotten thing to do," Ian agreed. The brothers had a lot of sympathy with any ordinary poacher. Not poaching gangs, of course. They were keen anglers themselves, if not very expert, and indeed fishing was their doctor father's favourite pastime. They had been brought up amongst anglers and talk of the sport. Their father could afford to pay for his fishing—but, with never very much pocket-money of their own, they could sympathise with any keen fisherman who could not afford the quite expensive charges of fishing for salmon. They had, in fact, fished in certain waters without due permission themselves, more than once—though that was just for brown trout, of course. It was not really poaching—but it was the same sort of thing.

The mention of the police set their new friend off into agitation again. "Keep the police outa this!" he said hoarsely. "I'm having nothing to do with the cops, d'you hear? They'd have me in the jail again, before I'd be spelling me name."

"Again . . . ?" Ian faltered.

"Och, they caught me once before, see, taking a fish.

I went to the jail then, and me with no money to pay the fine. I lost me job. I'm not wanting to lose the one I have now. So no police, see. They have me on their books."

"Oh, well . . ."

"Off with you now, and get me something to eat, for the love o' Mike!" the man urged. "And a drink. I'm drier than ever with all this talk. And mind—your promise by all that's holy that you'll not be telling a soul about me? Not a living soul, see?"

"Not even our aunt? If we're to get you food . . ." Ian objected.

"No aunts! Not on your life. None worse to talk than old dames. I want your promise."

The boys promised, rather reluctantly.

"Be off, then, for any sake. And remember the aspirins, now."

"It will take a while," Don pointed out. "We're five or six miles, here, from where we're staying at Denholm. We've got bikes—but we can't just turn up at our aunt's house, demand food and stuff, and come straight away again without explaining what we're doing. If we're not to tell her, it will have to be done carefully, or she'll ask questions."

"Okay, okay. Keep your auntie outa this." The man groaned, as he moved. "See—here's a pound note. Get the stuff in a shop. You can keep the change. But get back quick as you can. I'm trusting you, now."

"All right. We'll go. Good-bye, just now. And good luck."

"Luck!" the Irishman snorted. "Never had I a mite o' luck in all me born days!"

Up the steps and out again into the sunny afternoon, the twins stared at each other, blinking in the bright light.

"Well!" Don burst out. "Can you beat that? We seem to have landed ourselves into something, this time!"

"Yes. But what else could we do? The man's hurt. Needing help. We couldn't just leave him there, and forget him."

"No. Of course not. But all this secrecy, and avoiding the police and so on—perhaps legally we *shouldn't* be helping him?"

"I don't see why not. We're not doing any harm. He's suffered enough for poaching his salmon," Ian declared, always soft-hearted. "You can see his point about not bringing the police in. We're not judges. But he badly needs help, and we can help him. We *have* to."

"That's true. Anyway, we've promised. Come on, then—it's nearly four o'clock. We'll have to hurry if we're to get down to the shops, then back here, and home to Denholm in time for supper."

Over at the road and the bicycles, they looked back across the valley at the lonely tower on its ridge. Ian pointed.

"Houndswyre Tower—just another old peel!" he quoted. "All the same! Just a lot of mouldering old stones piled on top of each other!"

"Well—he's not a widow, at any rate!" Don retorted, jumping on to his bike.

CHAPTER TWO

DOUBTING SAMARITANS

THE sun was nearly setting behind the distant hills of Ettrick Forest and Tweedsmuir before Dan and Ian got back to Houndswyre Tower—much later than they had intended. This was because, being Wednesday, they found that it was early closing day for the village shops, and they had to cycle another four miles into the town of Rulekirk to make their purchases. Also, with some thought for the injured man's comfort, Ian had insisted on asking at a farm for a few old sacks. They could not carry these filled with straw, of course, on their bicycles; they would have to be stuffed at the tower.

For the first time, they actually saw their Irishman—for they had bought a small electric torch for him. Dirty, unshaven, and clearly looking far from his best, he turned out to be a youngish man with a great mop of red hair and very blue eyes, one of which was swollen up, almost closed, as from a blow. He was dressed in a stained and torn old blue jacket and muddy dungaree trousers, with a down-turned wellington boot still on one foot. The other foot was bare, showing a horribly inflamed and discoloured ankle.

. . . a youngish man with a great mop of red hair.

Although undoubtedly their friend was relieved to see them, his first reaction was to treat the brothers to a stream of abuse for being so long away—evidently he had feared that they had deserted him. It took a little while for his resentment to wear off. They could hardly be angry with him for this, for the man looked so knocked about and ill that they could only feel sympathy for him, lying there helpless, in pain, in the darkness.

They laid out their purchases before him, in this black pit that was clearly the tower's former prison cell; a narrow, vaulted cavern, part-hewn out of the rock of the ridge, about twelve feet long by six wide, walls glistening with damp. They had brought the sufferer a loaf of bread, half-a-pound of butter, some boiled ham, a packet of dates, a bottle of beer and some more chocolate. Also the electric torch, the aspirins and a roll of bandage. They had not forgotten the bottle of cold water. There was five shillings in change, which they declared they could not dream of accepting.

The man, after an enormous drink which two-thirds finished the bottle of beer, wolfed down great hunks of bread and ham, ignoring the butter. Ian, trying to remember his Boy Scouts' First Aid training, knelt down beside the injured man, soaked his handkerchief in cold water to make a damp pad, and bound it as tightly as he could round the sprained ankle with the bandage, to an accompaniment of muffled groans and munching and choking from the patient.

Meanwhile, Don took the sacks outside to fill them with dead leaves, last year's bracken, dry grass or whatever he could find. Two, well-filled to lie on, and two loosely packed to serve as quilts, ought to make a more comfortable bed than the bare damp floor.

When they were finished with these efforts on his behalf, the Irishman looked considerably better and more cheerful. He actually grinned at them—and he had an impish and rather attractive smile, like so many of his race.

"You're good dacent-like boys, the both o' you—and me thinking you'd gone off with me pound!" he said. "Och, I'll be fine now. Right as a king on his throne, bedad!"

"You'll hardly be that!" Ian pointed out. "But a little better, perhaps. I still think you should let us help you upstairs. You'd be far more comfortable up above somewhere, where it's dry and there's some light, than in this Black Hole of Calcutta!"

"Never a bit of it," the other told him determinedly. "Leave me be. I'm fine here. If you boys can come snooping about this old castle or whatever it is, other nosey-parkers can do the same. I'm safer down here. Nobody's going to look in here."

"Then you'd better not groan and mutter in your sleep!" Don warned him. "That's what made us come looking."

"Was I doing that, now? Sink me—that's bad! I'll have to watch it."

"Can you, when you're asleep?" Don asked seriously.

"Och, the aspirins will maybe help."

"Don—we'll have to go," Ian announced. "We're late for supper already. Aunt Mary will be getting worried. It will be dark before we get to Denholm—and we've no lights for our bikes."

"Yes. Well—you'll be all right for the night now, will you?" Don said. "By the way—what is your name? We've got to call you something."

"Just you call me Mickey Pat," the other told him. "And now—no stories to your auntie."

"No. We promised. Good night, then, Mickey Pat. I hope you have a sort of half-decent night."

"We'll come and see you to-morrow," Ian added. "Bring you some more food."

"Do that, boys. And some more beer. And look now—fetch me a newspaper. To-day's paper, see. I could do with something to read."

"All right. Good night."

"Good night, and may the dear saints in heaven bless the pair o' you. Bedad, yes—and don't forget the beer."

The brothers felt very guilty that evening in not being able to tell their Aunt Mary why they were so late or what they had been doing. And even more so next morning, when they asked for a particularly large picnic lunch to take with them, because they wanted to be away for the whole day, visiting the Brackenhope dam and other places. The old lady, however, did not seem in the least put out, doubtless being only too glad that her nephews were so well able to entertain themselves without much help from her.

They found that it was too early in the morning to buy beer—something to do with licensing hours they were told, which seemed rather ridiculous with the bottles standing on the grocer's counter. They had to take a bottle of cider instead—which the shopkeeper told them was much stronger, curiously enough. Then they called at the paper shop and bought *The Scotsman*, and set off for Houndswyre.

Despite all the comforts and improvements, Mickey Pat was not in any very good mood that forenoon. Cider, he objected—what sort of a drink for a man was that? They might as well have brought him ginger pop. And this wasn't the right paper. He'd told them yesterday's paper—Wednesday's, not Thursday's. It *was* Thursday to-day, wasn't it? He'd been lying there so long . . .

"Yes—this is Thursday," Don told him. "Naturally we bought to-day's paper. Why do you want yesterday's?"

"Perhaps he expects to read about his poaching adventure the night before?" Ian suggested.

"No, no—nothing o' the sort," Mickey Pat assured hurriedly. "Doesn't matter. This'll do. Och, my poor head. It's aching fit to burst. And my ankle's worse, too—for all your bandaging. Those aspirins were no good. I didn't sleep a wink last night—not a wink.

And I've got terrible cramps—och, just wicked. With lying here." Undoubtedly the patient was very sorry for himself this morning.

"Daddy—he's a doctor—always says that when people suddenly begin to complain about everything, they're getting better," Ian told him helpfully.

"Why not let us give you a hand—to walk about a little?" Don suggested. "You could lean on us. Get some exercise. It would help your cramp, at least, Mickey Pat."

"Didn't I tell you—I can't move?" the man exclaimed. "Not an inch. It's stuck here I am. D'you think I can go hopping about like a hen on a griddle?"

"With us to support you . . ."

"Nonsense, boy. And, see you—are you not going to bind up my poor ankle again? Another cold pad. D'you not want me to get better, at all? Would you have me lying here till my dying day—and that maybe not so far ahead, either, bedad!"

Smiling, Ian bent to renew the cold water treatment and bandage. "I thought you said your leg was the worse for my bandaging, Mickey Pat?" he pointed out.

The Irishman grinned then. "Och, never heed me. If you'd brought in some dacent-like beer instead of this stuff, I'd have been fine."

The boys left, after a little while, promising to look in at the tower on their way back from Brackenhope in the late afternoon. They left most of their picnic lunch for the victim, too.

It was as they were stepping out over the worn threshold into the bright morning again, that Don suddenly gripped Ian's arm, and pointed downwards at their feet. There, just outside the doorway, was a large patch of muddy bare earth. And imprinted on the mud, beside the tracks of their own crepe-soled sandals, were the clear footmarks, one pointing outwards, the other inwards, of a man-size wellington boot.

The boys stared from the tracks to each other.

"You see that?" Don whispered. "Look at that footprint. One boot only. And, see—there's a smudgy mark here. That will be made by his bare foot, just lightly set down. He's been outside, and come in again. This morning—for it rained last night. Only our footprints of this morning show."

"But . . . he said he couldn't move an inch! That he was stuck down there."

"I know. That's the point."

"It couldn't be somebody else? Not his tracks at all. Other people can wear wellingtons."

"Strange that only one boot shows. It's a left foot, too. It's Mickey Pat's right foot that's injured. There's something very fishy about this."

Tiptoeing carefully round the muddy patch, the brothers moved away until they were well out of hearing distance of the tower, and they could talk freely.

"It needn't be anything really fishy," Ian pointed out. "It's probably just a tiny thing, actually. You heard how sorry for himself he was, this morning. Piling it on about his aches and pains. He probably just exaggerates everything. Some Irishmen are supposed to be like that, aren't they? I mean, he just doesn't want to admit that he can hobble about a bit. Thinks he'll get more sympathy from us, this way."

"Perhaps," Don admitted. "Could be that. But why does he stay down in that cell, then? You'd think he'd at least let us help him up—maybe to the first floor, where it's dry and there's light, and he'd be more comfortable?"

"He's afraid, probably, that those keepers will still be looking for him. They might take a look into the tower—but not look down into that black hole. That's what he suggested."

"But if he's frightened about that, when he can hobble about even without our support, why doesn't he get us to help him right over to the road? It's not so terribly far. Then he could get away from here altogether—back to his home, wherever that is. Get a lift. Stop a car."

"Goodness knows . . ."

Puzzling it over in their minds, the twins went back to their bicycles, and set off on their day's run to Brackenhope, and if they had time, to the Ettrick valley. During the day, they came to the conclusion that, whatever it all meant, their friend Mickey Pat was worth watching carefully.

They had a good day at the new reservoir and its workings—at least, Don had, though Ian found it all rather less interesting. They were distinctly hungry before the end of it, and wishing that they had not been quite so generous with their picnic luncheon to Mickey Pat.

Coming back specially by the same route, in the early evening, they made another call at Houndswyre Tower. Carefully, before going in, they took a look at the muddy patch in front of the door. More footprints showed on the mud, though not so clearly now, for it was drying up. But the imprints were sufficiently visible to show that they were all the marks of one bar-soled left boot. Exchanging glances, they went inside and down into the pit.

Mickey Pat seemed to be dozing when they arrived, but declared that he was glad to see them. He was in good form to-night, even cracking jokes and announcing that in another couple of days he would be perfectly fit and away out of this dump. His only complaint was that the torch battery had gone flat. Would they get him another one? Also he wanted to write a letter; he needed paper and an envelope. And more food, of course. And not to forget to buy the beer to-night, during licensing hours. Better get a few bottles. He produced another pound note. For a hard-up poacher, he appeared to be less poverty-stricken than he had sounded.

Deliberately Don asked him if he did not now want a hand up, to climb to more comfortable quarters above. And again, almost angrily, they were told that

that was impossible, that he could not move. He was all right down here, anyway. Safer. Why were they so keen to get him upstairs?

The boys were sorely tempted to challenge the man with telling them untruths, to inform him that they knew that he could move about, and had in fact been outside the tower more than once. But they did not do so. There was some mystery here, and they felt that they were much more likely to get to the bottom of it by keeping their mouths shut and their eyes and ears open, than by antagonising this Mickey Pat.

They cycled back to Denholm that evening very thoughtfully indeed.

CHAPTER THREE

THE WRECKED CAR

"Does a lot of poaching go on, Aunt Mary? Round about here?" Don asked casually at supper in Lilac Cottage that night. "In the River Teviot and its tributaries, I mean?"

"Mercy me—I don't know, Don. Poaching? I shouldn't think so." Their aunt was a little, round, plump and comfortable lady, their mother's much older sister. She blinked at her nephews now, from behind rimless, spectacles. "You mean, poaching for fish?"

"Of course. For salmon."

"Goodness—how should I know, laddie? It's not the sort of thing I'd ever hear about . . ."

"You don't see it mentioned in the papers?" Ian put in.

"I can't say that I do. Why should I? Poaching salmon! Though, mind you, I shouldn't wonder at all. With all this crime going on. I've never heard the like. It never used to be this way when I was young. The Borders used to be an honest countryside. And now! Cars stolen. The post office at Jedwater broken into. And now this terrible thing of the Countess's jewels. That is quite shameful. Really, when it comes to Lady Borthwick's jewels . . . !"

Don was not interested in the Countess's jewels. "You don't think that poaching is actually common, then? I mean, if you've not heard about it, or seen it much mentioned in the newspapers here . . . ?"

"Och, I shouldn't think so. Mind, I don't know anything about it, really. But I'd have thought that the Teviot was too dirty, nowadays, too much polluted with that horrid grey stuff from the mills at Rulekirk, to have any salmon left in it. Could the beasts live in that?"

"That's what I thought myself," Don agreed. "It looks pretty foul. But there is another river that runs into the Teviot. Down a bit. Comes in from the north, you know. It joins the Teviot not far from that place they call Houndswyre. Where the old tower is. Would there be salmon in that, d'you think?"

"Goodness knows, Don. That will be the Swale Water, I think. I suppose that there might be salmon in that. But what's all this about? Are you two wanting to go fishing? For salmon? You're too young laddies—och, you're much too young. You might be pulled right in, mercy on us! They can be real big fish, salmon. You'll have to leave that until you're a good bittie older, see you . . ."

"It's not that, at all, Auntie . . ."

"Will they have keepers on this river? This Swale.

Or bailiffs, don't they call them?" Ian asked. "To keep poachers away?"

"Dearie me, I wouldn't have thought so. I would think that would be a great waste of time. And men." Their aunt shook her head and pursed her lips. "If the earl has men to spare, I'd say he'd be a lot better having them looking after his own house and his pretty wife's jewels, than bothering about a few silly fish! But, mind, Don—I'm serious what I say about no salmon fishing. For you two, I mean. While you're in my care, I'm not having you take any stupid risks. And if you were thinking of trying *poaching*—then just think again, the pair of you! Mercy to goodness, don't you consider such a thing . . . !"

"Of course not. It's not that at all, Auntie. This earl . . . ? You mean the river, the Swale, belongs to some lord or other?"

"Of course it does. They all do. Och, boy—half this countryside belongs to the Earl of Borthwick. Surely you know that. Always has done. One of the oldest families in all the Borders . . ."

"It was the Borthwicks who built Houndswyre Tower, wasn't it?" Ian put in.

> "Cruel Borthwick, black be your fall,
> May your lady weep on your castle wall!"

"My, my—fancy you knowing that old rhyme, Ian! I haven't heard that since I was a lassie at the school.

But that was a long, long time ago. I mean, about the Borthwicks being cruel. The earl's a very nice gentleman. And the Countess—my, she couldn't be nicer. Bonny, too. She opened the church sale just a month ago. Poor thing, to lose all those lovely jewels. Family heirlooms, too, some of them, they say. Absolutely priceless. What this country's coming to, I do not know! Just think of it. Taken right out of her own bedroom! It's a disgrace, that's what it is. They say that the famous Borthwick diamond necklace is worth £20,000 in itself! Can you imagine that? It will be insured, I suppose. But still . . ."

"Yes, Auntie. But about this Swale Water," Don persisted. "D'you think this Earl of Borthwick will have a lot of gamekeepers on it? To preserve his fishing?"

"Well, he might, I suppose. Not just for the fishing, though, I'd think. More like his pheasants and things. It's not far there, from his big mansion. Swaleholm House. Where the robbery was."

"Have gamekeepers any right to use force? Violence? I mean, to strike people that might be poaching. Or . . ."

Ian interrupted. "When was this robbery, Aunt Mary?"

"Why, laddie—haven't I been telling you. It was all in the papers, yesterday. Did you not see it? So it must have been the night before. Tuesday night. There was a big party at Swaleholm House that night, and while it was going on these horrid thieves broke in . . ."

"Two nights ago!" Ian said. "M'mmm." He looked at Don.

"And this Swaleholm is not far from, from . . . !"

As with one accord the boys changed the subject.

"How long will you want us for, to-morrow morning, at Rulekirk, Aunt Mary?" Don asked. "At this market?"

"I've decided not to go in the morning, after all," the old lady told them. "I'd forgotten—there's a church coffee morning in the village here to-morrow, and I'd said I'd go. We'll just go in to Rulekirk in the afternoon. Probably not so busy then, anyway. And afterwards, perhaps we might pay a visit to the cinema. You'd like that, wouldn't you?"

The brothers exchanged glances. This meant altering their plans. They would enjoy going to the pictures, of course. But they had told Mickey Pat that they would not be up to the tower until the late afternoon, next day. Still it would not make any real difference.

It was their aunt who reverted to the subject of fish. "Why were you two so interested in salmon, all of a sudden?" she wondered.

"Oh, it's nothing, really," Don assured. "Just a sort of idea we had. But don't worry, Auntie—we're not thinking of doing any poaching!"

"I should say not! Not while you're with me, my lads!"

"It's just that we're interested in fishing generally," Ian put in. "Daddy being such a keen angler. We do a bit of it ourselves, you know. Not salmon, of course. Just brown trout . . ."

"Och, that's different. I once caught a brown trout myself. Long ago, mind. I had it for my breakfast, in oatmeal. If it's just some trouties you'd like to catch you should go and see Dod Pringle. He's the man does the most fishing in Denholm. He'd tell you where to go. Dod Pringle, the blacksmith . . ."

"Oh, I don't think we need bother him, Auntie . . ."

Ian interrupted. "We might just have a word with him in the morning," he said. " Just in case . . ."

"Do that," Aunt Mary nodded. "He's a nice man, and an elder of the kirk."

Later, up in their own room, the twins could speak plainly.

"I'm beginning to wonder about Mickey Pat—really wonder," Don declared. "I don't believe, you know, that keepers did all that to him, at all. Injured him like that, I mean. I've been thinking about it a lot. If they did catch him and gave him a bit of a hiding first, they would still want to hand him over to the police, wouldn't they? So they wouldn't knock him about so badly that the police would be bound to ask questions about it. Even if they were that sort of tough types. Which doesn't seem very likely, does it?

And anyway, how could he escape from them, damaged like that, with such a bad ankle? The ankle injury is genuine enough—even though he can walk better than he pretends. He could never get away from a number of them, crippled like that."

"I thought of that, too. If they were as tough with him as all that, surely they wouldn't just let him go, afterwards? And it seemed strange, from the first, that they should have been so savage with him. He said they got the fish and did all this to him. But he got away. And hid himself, in some bushes. Four of them. Big men."

"D'you think this Swale Water will be important enough to have four keepers and bailiffs patrolling it? That's what I was getting at, to Aunt Mary. I think it's too small. Not really a salmon river at all. And the Teviot looks too dirty . . ."

"He didn't actually say that it was in the Swale, of course. Or the Teviot, either. He just said out of the river. I suppose it might be some other river?"

"But he said he'd dragged himself there. To the tower. And that it was a bad business getting there. As it would be, goodness, with a leg like that! So it could only have been the Swale, surely. Anyway, there's no other river round about there, is there? No other tributary that he could have hobbled away from? Not that we've seen."

"No. And it's not as though it was the Tweed—where we know there are lots of bailiffs." Ian paused.

"You heard what Auntie said? About this jewel robbery. It took place on the same night as Mickey Pat's poaching fight. D'you think . . . d'you think that there could be any connexion? I mean, it's a bit of a coincidence, isn't it?"

Don shook his curly head. "I thought of that, too. But I don't really see why there should be. Mickey Pat looks much more like a poacher than a jewel thief! People who steal valuable jewellery aren't likely to be Mickey Pat's type, I'd think. He's no professional cracksman, that! Or if he is, all the thrillers we've read, and the TV plays we've seen, have been away out! Anyway, why should he have been beaten up, in that case? Nobody was caught, at the robbery, from what Auntie says."

"No. That's true. But I still don't think keepers would do all that," Ian objected. "I think it might just be worth seeing this man, this fisherman that Auntie told us about. Dod somebody-or-other—the blacksmith. He'd be able to give us a better idea about salmon fishing possibilities in the area, and bailiffs and so on."

"Agreed. No harm in that."

So, next morning, the two boys made their way, before heading for the shop to buy Mickey Pat's provisions, to the smiddy on the green. Here they found the blacksmith, Dod Pringle, not shoeing a horse as would have been suitable, but underneath an intricate piece of farm machinery, all teeth and prongs, with an oxy-acetylene cylinder and blow-lamp, mask over face. They did not interrupt him until he came crawling out. Don took the lead, as usual.

"Good morning," he said. "We are staying with Miss Turnbull, at Lilac Cottage. She's our aunt, actually. And she told us to come to you to ask about fishing. She says you know a lot about that sort of thing . . . ?"

Dod Pringle was not as big and brawny as the village blacksmiths that the boys had read about, but he looked keen-witted and quite pleasant. "Och, aye—I ken you fine," he told them. "You'll be Miss Jean's laddies, doon from Edinburgh. Leastways, she used to be Miss Jean. She married a doctor, I mind. MacDonald, was it no'?"

"That's right. We're Don and Ian MacDonald. We're . . . we're rather interested in salmon fishing. I don't mean that we want to do any ourselves, you know. Just to know about it. Our father is a great angler. Maybe you could tell us . . . ?"

"Salmon, is it? Och, well—there's no' an awfu' lot o' salmon caught roond about here nowadays, mind . . ."

"There's not? That's what we wanted to know."

"It was different in my young days. Then there was plenty o' salmon in the Teviot. But, och, the mills ruined it. What it is they put into the watter I dinna ken, but I dinna blame the salmon for keeping awa', and that's a fact. Dirty greasy stuff. Something oot o' the wool, I suppose—some dye, maybe. Anyway, it's a long whilie since anyone fished for salmon within ten mile o' Rulekirk."

"M'mmm. We rather thought that. What about the tributary river? The Swale Water, down near Houndswyre? Would there be salmon in that?"

"The Swale? Och, there might be the odd fish. But no' many. It's ower wee. No' enough watter in it, most times."

"But there *could* be salmon in it?" That was Ian.

"I reckon there might be, yes. The Teviot's got sort o' diluted by then. I mean there's been a lot o' burns coming into it, to freshen the watter up again, by the time you get down to the Swale. So salmon might come up that far from the Tweed. One or two. And they might turn up into the Swale."

"I see. But it's not what you'd call a salmon river?"

"Sakes, no, laddie! Far from it. I've never heard o' a salmon being taken oot o' it, and that's a fact."

"Then . . . then there are not likely to be bailiffs patrolling it? Or keepers?"

"Guidness me—what for would they dae that?"

"Well, we just sort of wondered."

"Na, na—they'd never put bailiffs on the Swale. Yon would be plain daft."

"But keepers? Gamekeepers? Could there be gamekeepers there? It belongs to this Lord Borthwick, doesn't it?"

"Och, well—aye, there could be keepers aboot there. The Swale runs through the earl's lands—runs roond his policies, in fact. He has two-three keepers, right enough. But I wouldna think they'd be bothering that much aboot the river. It would be the game—the pheasants and partridges and the like. But . . . what's a' this in aid of, laddies? You thinking o' trying to fish the Swale? You dinna have to bother aboot keepers, guidsakes! Just you phone up the earl's factor, and he'll gie you permission to fish, any time. For trouts, that is. He's decent enough aboot letting folk fish. But no' for salmon, likely. No' that you'd catch any there, anyway, I'd think."

"No. I mean, thank you. Yes, we'll remember about the factor. We weren't really actually thinking of fishing ourselves. Not just now. Just . . . well, making inquiries. You've told us just what we need. It's kind of you, Mr. Pringle. Many thanks."

Don was in a hurry to get away now.

"No trouble, laddies. Always interested to help anybody aboot fishing. Gie your mither my regards."

Safely round at the other side of the green, near the grocer's shop, the twins got into a huddle.

"Well—*that's* pretty clear!" Don said. "It's all a yarn. Mickey Pat's been having us on."

"Well—we still can't be absolutely certain," Ian pointed out. "It's not been bailiffs, that's obvious.

But it is still just possible that he'd been caught by keepers. Perhaps it wasn't salmon at all that he was poaching—but game. Pheasants and partridges."

"But why should he say salmon, then? I mean, if he admits poaching one thing what's the point in not admitting it was game? I can't see any sense in it. It's no worse a crime to poach pheasants than salmon, is it?"

"No-o-o. I suppose not. All that we can say is that, though it almost certainly was not because of salmon poaching, he *could* have had a fight with Lord Borthwick's keepers." Ian stopped. "I say—suppose he *had* been poaching game, and these keepers were out that night, not looking for poachers, but for the jewel robbers! They might have caught him lurking about the big house, and in trying to escape, there was a fight? Isn't that possible?"

"Well, yes. But it still doesn't explain why he says that he was poaching salmon."

"No. Well, we'll just have to accept that he's not telling us the whole truth. Maybe, if we let him see that we realise he's lying, he will explain properly. It's about all that we can do, anyway."

So, presently, laden with two bottles of light beer, some rolls, more boiled ham, and a big slab of currant cake, they set off on their bicycles down fair Teviotdale.

In due course they arrived up at the lonely Houndswyre Tower determined to ask some carefully probing questions, having discussed the attitude that they ought to take up, on the way. They decided that they would be perfectly friendly and civil, but would not be put off either by Irish blarney or with obviously false stories. After all, if they were going to go on helping this man, they were entitled to know what had happened to him, what he had been up to. It might not be easy to get the whole truth out of him —but it was time that they tried.

It was not easy, indeed. For when they clambered down into the underground cell, it was to find that Mickey Pat was not there. The sacks of grass and bracken lay where he had left them, some empty paper bags were scattered about and the bottle of water stood in a corner—and that was all. They had seen no sign of him round about the tower, of course, as they came over from the road—and it was a bare ridge where anyone near at hand would have been obvious.

"Well, I'm blowed!" Don exploded. "He's gone. Done a bunk! Just cleared off. Of all the nerve . . . !"

"Maybe not," Ian said. "He's maybe still about somewhere. Up above, perhaps. On one of the upper floors. As we suggested before . . ."

They hurried up the narrow corkscrew stone stairway of the tower, tripping on the worn and broken steps, looking in at the room on each floor. Right up to the ruinous and dangerous battlements, seventy feet above the rock itself, they went—without any sign of Mickey Pat. There was a magnificent view from the parapet-walk, out over all Teviotdale to the great range of the Cheviot Hills beyond, that formed the border between Scotland and England—but the boys did not even glance at it all. They searched the scene much nearer at hand—for a lone figure that limped. But without success.

"Well, I think that's pretty mean," Don declared. "Just to cut off, without leaving us any word at all. If he couldn't wait to tell us, for some reason, he might at least have left a note . . ."

"I don't suppose he could do that. He asked us to bring him paper and envelope, remember. So he probably had nothing to write on. Still, it's a bad show if he's just gone off without waiting for a word with us. But he's a pretty weird character, of course."

They went down again to the tower doorway. It had been dry overnight, and the muddy patch was caked hard, revealing only old footmarks. There was nothing to be learned there.

"Well—what now?" Ian asked. "Nothing for it, I suppose, but just to go back to Denholm. Or should we wait a bit? Hang around here in case he comes back? That might be sensible."

"I suppose we should do that. He *might* be intending to return."

"Yes. Remember, Don, we did say that we wouldn't be here to-day until late afternoon. Because we were going in to the market at Rulekirk in the morning with Auntie. We know that Mickey Pat moves about more than he admits. Possibly he went a bit farther, this time, thinking that we wouldn't be coming for hours yet."

"M'mmm. Maybe. But it's a bit of a bore just to hang around here, waiting. Perhaps we should just do something else, for a bit. Go somewhere, and come back later." Don paused. "I know. We could go over there, to the north, and have a look at this Swale Water. Obviously it curves round in that deep dip over there, not very far away. We'd get a better idea of the whole position, and how much chance there is likely to be that he *was* poaching, whether salmon or game."

"Yes. We could do that. Maybe we could try and see where this Swaleholm House lies, too. Check up on the whole position. We may be glad of knowing it all, if we're going to challenge Mickey Pat. Better than just waiting here, anyway."

They descended the Houndswyre ridge on the farther, north side now, and crossed some more of the sheep-dotted pasture, all outcropping rock and yellow-flowering gorse bushes. In front of them the land sank suddenly and clearly away into the long curve of a deep and wooded valley.

They were following a sheep-path. Abruptly, Don, in the lead, stopped, and pointed. In a spot where the path was worn down to bare soil, the mark of a rubber-soled boot was clearly imprinted. A left foot again, obviously the same bar-soled boot as they had seen at the tower doorway. The muddy patch was long enough to have shown a second boot-print if there had been one for the other foot. There was only a blurred smudge mark, and the pointed little hole clearly made by a stick. The footprint was not new, either; the mud was caked hard. It had not been made that morning.

"So-o-o!" Ian said. "This isn't the first time that he's been going quite a long distance from the tower. That would be yesterday's, at least. Despite all his talk of lying close, and terrible pain, and all that. I wonder what he's up to?"

"Time we found out," Don answered.

This point was about three hundred yards from the tower, and not very far ahead, between the end of their grassy, gently-sloping hillside and the beginning of the steeply-dropping woods of the valley, the boys found a road that they had not known about. Hidden by a hedge on their side, it was really not much more than a narrow winding country lane, with even a little spine of grass growing along the crown of it in many places, showing that it was but little used by motor traffic at least. Crossing it, they leaned over a low stone wall at the far side, moss-grown and broken-down, to look down the steep slope beyond.

A good distance below them, probably more than a hundred feet, a clear shallow stream curved. It was bigger than a burn but hardly large enough to call a river. Perhaps twenty feet across, it chuckled and twinkled on its way. The bank between them and it was grown with a scattering of old trees, ash and oak mainly, with not much undergrowth. And beyond the stream was flattish meadowland dotted with thorn trees, where cattle grazed.

"From here it certainly doesn't look big enough, deep enough, for salmon," Don said. "I'm sure the blacksmith was right. Not worth poaching."

"There may be pools, of course," Ian pointed out, but doubtfully. "We can't see much of it from here, with it curving round both ways." He looked farther afield. "I wonder which way Swaleholm House lies?"

They turned right-handed along the road, to see what the Swale looked like from farther downstream, when Ian stopped.

"Listen!" he said. "What's that?"

Distinctly above the natural sounds of the valley, the murmur of the river, the singing of birds and the baaing of sheep, they heard a faint clanging noise, repeated. It was like hammering on metal. It did not seem to come from very far away.

"I wonder what that is?"

"There's no sign of any houses or buildings around here. Except the tower itself," Don pointed out. "It's somebody banging on something like tin. It's coming from back the way—upstream."

"Yes. D'you think it could be Mickey Pat?"

The boys turned and went walking in the opposite direction. After a bit, round a sharp bend in the winding road, they could hear the clanging sound more clearly. It stopped and started, and seemed to be coming up to them from the depth of the valley.

"Look at that wall." Ian pointed suddenly. "That's been knocked over, recently. See—there's skid marks here. A car's gone into that wall. It must . . . it must have gone right over!"

The brothers hurried to the edge of the steep slope, where a few scattered stones were all that remained of the already somewhat tumbledown wall. They peered over and down, once more, through the trees.

At the foot of the bank, half-in and half-out of the river, a car lay upside down, wheels in the air. Its path down the slope was easily traced by scrapes and scores and broken bushes. Bending over it, tugging at it, was Mickey Pat.

CHAPTER FOUR

SOMETHING A-MISSING

"GOODNESS—there's been an accident!" Don cried. "Look at that car! Come on! Quick!"

"Heavens! And we've been blaming poor Mickey Pat! He must have heard the crash. Come to try and help . . ."

The boys went scrambling and slithering down the steep slope, grabbing at trees and undergrowth to control their descent. With his bad ankle, the Irishman must have found it most difficult to climb down.

Bending and tugging and banging at the overturned car, Mickey Pat did not notice the twins' approach until they were almost upon him. Then hearing them, he looked up and back, and for a moment his jaw dropped. He gazed at them, part of an upholstered seat half-out of the window of the vehicle, pulling at it.

"Is anybody hurt?" Don gasped. "Are you trying to get somebody out?"

"This is awful!" Ian panted. "What's happened? Is he . . . is the driver . . . in there?"

Mickey Pat merely stared at them, frowning and biting his lip.

"He's not . . .? He's not . . . ?" Ian couldn't bring himself to say the word.

"Is he still inside?" Don demanded.

"No," the Irishman said shortly. That was all.

"Not there?" Don stepped forward to peer into the car. "Where is he, then? You don't mean that . . . that he's in the river? Drowned?"

Mickey Pat shook his head. He was supporting himself against the vehicle, keeping the weight off his ankle. For so voluble an individual, he seemed very wordless. Shaken, no doubt.

"What happened?" Ian demanded again. He, too, peered into the capsized car. Clearly it was empty, although in a mess inside, with everything scattered about, upholstery torn and stuffing strewn around. Broken glass lay on what had been the inside of the roof.

Mickey Pat found his voice. "Bedad, you can see what happened, can't you? What d'you think? The blamed car came down the bank."

"Yes. But what's happened to the driver?"

"The driver? Eh? Och . . . search me! He's gone. Gone. You can see that, too, now can't you?" Mickey Pat sounded not at his best. No doubt he was in much pain, having hobbled and clambered down all this way. "Och, you boys not got eyes in your heads?"

"Yes. But . . . this is very queer!" Don said. "I mean, for him to have disappeared like this." He looked back, up the bank, on either hand. There was no sign of anybody lying there, and the hillside was fairly clear. "Do you think we should search the undergrowth? There's not a lot of it. I suppose he might have been thrown clear as it came rolling down."

"We'd see him, surely, from this angle," Ian pointed out. "It's all pretty open."

The Irishman said nothing, but began to push the car seat back inside the body again.

"He's perhaps dazed. Half-stunned. Injured," Don suggested. "He may have wandered away, not really knowing what he was doing. Trying to get help. It must have been awful, coming through that wall, down that slope, banging against those trees. Goodness! How long ago was it, Mickey Pat? When it happened? Did you hear it up at the tower?"

The man shook his head. "Och, I don't know, at all," he muttered. "I . . . och, my poor head!" He put a hand up to his brow, and then sat down suddenly against the overturned chassis. "By the blessed saints—my leg!"

Perplexed, the brothers looked at him, and then at each other.

"You've hurt yourself more?" Ian sympathised. "Bound to have done. You shouldn't have come, really. Not in your state. Look, Don—don't you think we ought to get him back to the tower right away. Then we can come back and search for the driver of this car. Or maybe go and notify the police, straight away. One of us could . . ."

"Sure and you'll do no such thing!" Mickey Pat declared, surprisingly strongly, rousing himself. "Did I not tell the pair o' you—you're not bringing any policemen round about here! You are not!"

"But this is different," Don protested. "There's been an accident. It's serious. We've got to let the police know. A man may be lying about anywhere, unconscious perhaps. There may be more than one. Seriously hurt. We've got to do something. The police must be informed. It won't be linked with . . . with your business, in any way."

"Nonsense, boy! The police, bad cess to them, will have been informed long ago, to be sure. There's never a bit of need to inform them again. And, sure they'd link it with me, bedad! Nothing surer . . ."

The twins stared.

"Long ago?" Don said. "You say they will have been informed long ago?"

"How could they have been?" Ian demanded. "What d'you mean?"

"Mercy on us—use your eyes, will you!" the other told them. "This car's been here for days, hasn't it?"

Don and Ian looked at each other, mystified.

"For days? How do you know that?"

"Och, look at the marks. See for yourselves."

It was true enough. When the boys examined the scars on the bank and the damage to the trees, they could see that they were not in fact new. They had been rained upon, for one thing, obviously—and it had not rained since the night before last. Moreover, the mud on the upturned base of the car was caked dry and hard.

"Then . . . then you didn't hear it? Hear it from the tower, and come hurrying?" Ian challenged the Irishman.

"I didn't say I heard anything, now, did I?"

"No-o-o. I suppose not. I'm sorry. But . . . how *did* you find it? How did you know to come here, in the first place? All this way. And down that hill. With your bad leg?"

Mickey Pat looked from one to the other, not very affectionately, and ran a dirty hand through his red hair. "Och, well, I felt better this morning, see. A lot better. So I reckoned I'd be trying out my ankle, see. Have a little small walk. Thought I'd come this way. To have a look at the river. Where I was poaching, see. Maybe some o' my gear dropped. In the fight. Nets and such-like. Then . . . I saw this." He looked at the car, and groaned, and leaning forward suddenly put his head between his hands. "Och, but mercy on us, it's been too much for me! Too much altogether, by the powers! I shouldn't have come, at all. You'll have to be helping me back to the ould castle, boys, so you will? It's the fool I was to have come . . ."

"But you've been out walking before this," Don began. "We know that . . ."

"Yes—and what you've told us isn't just exactly right. I mean, there are things that need explaining," Ian added. It was an uncomfortable business telling a man to his face that he was a liar. "There's quite a few questions that we'd like to . . ."

"Oh, my ankle! It's killing me, d'you hear?" the sufferer interrupted. "And my head. It's splitting, that's what it is. I can't see for the pain of it. Where are you?" He groped out with his hands towards them.

The brothers sighed. Obviously nothing was to be got out of Mickey Pat just now. There seemed to be nothing for it but to help him back to Houndswyre Tower.

They took an arm each, and between them aided the man to his feet—or to one foot rather. Then giving him all the support that they could, and seeking to pick out the easiest route up the hill, they began to climb with him up the steep bank.

Mickey Pat may have been a born actor—but there was no doubt that he suffered greatly on the slow, painful journey back to the tower. His groans and exclamations were unceasing—and his language lurid—but much of it was forced out from between his clenched teeth. His ankle might not have been quite so agonising as he pretended, but there was no question that it was badly sprained. His bruised ribs were hurting him too, for sometimes when he stumbled—which was not seldom—a spasm of pain twisted his face. And yet, somehow, as the boys could not help reminding themselves, he had got himself down to the river on his own.

At last they got him up the bank, over the road, and across the rising pasture-land. The final ascent to the tower itself was deadly slow, with the man panting, biting his lips, and sweat streaming down his face. This was no play-acting. He was leaning heavily on his supporters now. He almost fell down the few steps into the dark cell, and practically collapsed on his stuffed sacks therein, gasping and moaning.

At a loss, the twins peered at each other in the gloom of that place. They had had every intention of questioning him, of telling him of their suspicions and demanding explanations; but it hardly seemed decent to try to do so now. It was doubtful, indeed, whether he was in any state to answer them at the moment. In fact, he did not reply when they spoke to him. By unspoken consent they decided to leave their questions for another occasion.

They did the best for the sufferer that they could, meantime. Don fitted the new battery for the torch. Ian, taking off the dirty bandage, put on a fresh cold-water pad, and tied up the still very swollen ankle. Undoubtedly to-day's activities had made it worse. The patient raised his head for long enough to gulp down some of the new supply of beer, spilling some of it down his unshaven chin in the process—but he did not seem interested in the food for the time being. He closed his eyes, and made it most obvious that he wanted only to be left alone.

Looking down at him, the brothers sighed, and Don switched off the torch.

"The best thing is just to get some sleep, I think," Ian told him. "You'll probably feel better after that. There's food here, and more beer. But . . . well, you've most likely set yourself back a day or two with that ankle, Mickey Pat."

There was no reply.

"We won't be back again to-day, I'm afraid," Don mentioned. "It's a pity, rather. We've got to go to Rulekirk with our aunt this afternoon. Instead of this morning. We won't be home until late." It seemed somewhat unkind to tell the victim that they were going to enjoy themselves at the cinema. "But we'll come again early to-morrow, to see how you are getting on. Is that all right?"

A groan was all their answer.

"We hope you'll tell us some things that are rather worrying us, then," Ian added.

Silence.

"Well, all the best, Mickey Pat."

Strangely, they felt almost guilty leaving the man in that dark and unpleasant hole, alone, when he was in such evident pain. As they went out into the sunlight, and back across the valley towards their bicycles, they told themselves how foolish they they were to feel so, of course. If there was anybody should be feeling that way, it should be Mickey Pat, surely?

"Mind you, fair's fair—but I'm sure he's piling it on a bit," Don said. "All that moaning and groaning. I'll bet that it's largely that he doesn't want to answer any questions until he's had time to think up convincing answers. He was pretty shaken when he saw us, down there at the car."

"Maybe, yes. But he's bound to be in great pain too, you know," the soft-hearted Ian argued. "That ankle is bad. I just don't know how he got as far as the river with it, in the first place. It must have been a ghastly trip, however slowly he took it."

"What I want to know is *why*? I think that he knew that the car was there. Maybe he'd seen it before—when he had been out on another of his secret walks. If it's been there for some time."

"Why didn't he tell us, then?"

"He couldn't have done—without admitting that he could walk a lot better than he pretended."

"No. But what's the point in it all? Why pretend that he could not walk? Where does it get him?"

"Goodness knows. I don't know why he stays at the tower at all, if he can walk as far as the river. It's not as though it was a very comfortable place. He could have walked to the road, here. And got a lift to wherever he lives. I can't make head nor tail of it all."

"Presumably he doesn't want to go back home. For some reason or other. Maybe he thinks the police will be looking for him there."

"Well, he could go *somewhere* else, surely? Better than this cold old ruin."

"It's a good hide-out, if he doesn't want to be found. I mean, until he is fit enough to make a quick getaway . . ."

The twins were half-way back to Denholm, free-wheeling down the long hill towards the Teviot, when suddenly Ian remembered something. He shouted, and put on his brakes.

"Don!" he cried. "We've forgotten the paper. The envelope. It's still in my pocket. For his letter, that he wanted to write."

They stopped.

"It doesn't really matter, does it?" Don said. "It will do to-morrow, won't it?"

"Well—we promised, you know. He said he wanted to send a letter. And to-morrow is Saturday. So if he's in a hurry with it, that means it will lie in some post-box until Monday, if he doesn't write to-day. I think we'd better go back."

"What a bore!" Don grumbled. "I reckon that's being just too fussy."

"We promised," Ian insisted. "He may have a wife or a mother or somebody, just waiting to hear from him. Somebody very anxious. And we're going to enjoy ourselves at the pictures . . ."

"Oh, all right. Come on, then," groaned Don. They turned back, to push their bicycles up the long hill again.

When they reached Houndswyre Tower once more, it was to find it empty. Mickey Pat had vanished.

CHAPTER FIVE

Two-and-Two Make . . . ?

"Well, I'm . . . I'm blowed!" Don exclaimed. "Gone! Can you beat that? He's done a bunk again. After all that. After all the moaning and the groaning. He sounded as though he was at death's door! And now . . . !"

Ian swallowed, and shook his head. "This is crazy!" he said. "Utterly crazy. How long have we been away? Not more than three-quarters of an hour. He can't have been feeling so much better in that time. Whether or not he was partly shamming, he *was* in real pain. All that sweat running down his face. He couldn't have faked that. He was in no state to go off walking again—that's certain. So soon. He must just have waited until we were safely away, and then scrammed, bad leg, ribs and all. It must have taken him a tremendous effort. What on earth has come over the man?"

"Something mighty fishy," Don asserted. "I wonder if he's gone for good, this time? I almost hope he has. I'm getting a bit tired of Mickey Pat. It's too one-sided a business this, altogether. He's just making fools of us—and making use of us, too."

They had a box of matches now, and struck a light. It showed that some of the food was gone, but some was still there. One of the beer bottles was empty, but the other was untouched.

"Looks as though he was coming back, all right," Ian said. "He wouldn't have left any of the beer if he was off for good, our Mickey Pat! I wonder, now . . . ?"

"D'you think . . . ? D'you think he's just done the same thing again, Ian? Gone away back to that wrecked car?" Don demanded.

"That's what I was wondering. It seems utterly daft. After the trouble he had getting back here. But . . . where else would he go, in such a hurry?"

"Goodness knows. But he *has* gone, somewhere. And we know that he was mighty interested in that car, for some reason or other. Remember the bangings we heard . . . ?"

"Come on—let's go and see."

The twins hurried downhill again, off to the north, and over to the narrow side road, hurrying along it north-westwards. They came to the spot where the wall was knocked down, and peered over.

Mickey Pat was down there. Indeed he was on his hands and knees beside the overturned car, with his head and shoulders actually inside, through a broken window.

"W-e-e-el!" Don said. "What d'you make of that, eh?" He did not realise it, but he whispered his question.

"I don't know. I can't think," Ian answered. "But whatever it is, it's mighty important. To him. That's obvious. He seems to be looking for something, doesn't he? Inside that car."

"Yes. And I think that is what he was doing before, when we interrupted him. He was searching. Not for a driver. For something else. Presumably he hasn't found whatever it was. And he's gone back, just as soon as we were out of the way. In spite of the pain."

"But what could it be? What could be all that important? Remember, he had half a seat dragged out, before."

"And there was a lot of hair-stuffing from the upholstery lying scattered around. I shouldn't think that even tumbling and rolling down this steep bank would do that—tear the leather inside and pull out the stuffing. Would you? I wonder if Mickey Pat did that himself? If he did, then he must be looking for something that had been hidden, and lost. Something pretty small."

"But . . . look, if so, then he must know this car. All about it. I say—it couldn't be his *own* car, could it?" Ian asked, a little breathlessly. "He said that it had been there for days. If it was his own, that would account for there being no driver to be found. And that it has been left lying there. And the police, therefore, would know nothing about it. If no accident had been reported, it could lie down there for long enough, and nobody ever notice it. Unless they were actually looking for something, and peered over here specially. It's steep down there, and part hidden. And this road is obviously seldom used. There doesn't seem to be any houses anywhere near . . ."

"M'mmm. I suppose that's right enough." Don sounded doubtful. "But . . . it looked to me a pretty good sort of car. Big. Expensive-looking. It's a Humber, isn't it? I didn't take any special note—but I seem to remember that's what it was. You can hardly tell, can you, from here? With it upside down?"

"Yes. It's one of those big Humber shooting-brakes. I noticed that. Not an old one, either, I don't think . . ."

"Well, goodness—our Mickey Pat isn't likely to own one of those, is he? They must be terribly expensive."

"Yes. I mean, no. He wouldn't own one—but he might have been *driving* one, just the same. He needn't be the owner. It could be his boss's car. If he was the driver, that could account for all his injuries. His damaged ankle and bruised ribs and black eye. Much more likely than being beaten up by keepers!"

"By Jove, yes! That's more like it. I think you've got something there, Ian. The more I think about it, the less I believe in this poaching-and-keepers story. Perhaps you've got it." Don gripped his brother's arm excitedly. "Perhaps that's what he's so scared about. Maybe he took a loan of his employer's car, without permission, and then went and had an accident and wrecked it? That would put him in a real jam. He

Mickey Pat had now backed out of the car.

wouldn't want the police inquiring into it, or finding him . . ."

"But what's he looking for inside the car, in that case?" Ian demanded. "Tearing the seating apart. Just having run off with his boss's car wouldn't make him do that. What's the point in him being so interested in it now?"

"I can't think what that's in aid of," Don admitted. "Something he left in the car when the accident happened. I suppose. And now he can't find it."

Mickey Pat had now backed out of the car, and was sitting beside it on the grass of the river's edge, obviously panting and exhausted, his head leaning against the dark red paintwork. Even from all this distance he looked the picture of dejection.

"He's in pain—you can see that," Don pointed out. "Whatever it is that he has lost, it means almost everything to him . . ."

"Listen, Don!" Ian interrupted urgently. "Suppose it's worse, much worse than we thought! Suppose that it's not just his boss's car that he has taken a loan of. Suppose it's a *stolen* car?"

"Oh, I say! But . . . what of it? I mean, what difference would that make, anyway?"

"The jewel robbery, of course!" Ian whispered.

"Whe-e-ew! Gosh—you don't really think . . . think that Mickey Pat? . . . Och, Ian—he isn't that sort of man. Not a real criminal, I mean."

"How do we know? We don't really know very

much about what real criminals look like, do we? We haven't actually met any. Except those deer poachers in the Highlands. The one that caught us was a nasty piece of work, certainly—much nastier than Mickey Pat. But we don't know that they were real criminals, either. Not professionals, I mean. And a big jewel robbery would take that sort, wouldn't it?" Ian shrugged. "It's just a thing we don't know. But . . . it all seems to work out, doesn't it?"

"I suppose it does. Sort of. Look—there he's creeping back inside the car again. He's determined enough—I'll say that for him."

"Yes. If there's a £20,000 diamond necklace in there somewhere, you could understand it, too!"

"My goodness! That's a thought."

Ian grabbed his brother's arm in his excitement. "It could all add up, Don. He could have pinched the countess's jewels at this Swaleholm House. Apparently it's not far from here. Then stolen one of the party guest's cars. He could have hidden the jewels in the upholstery somewhere, in case he was stopped or questioned. He'd keep off the main roads, where there might be police blocks when the alarm went off. He'd come bashing along this little-used side road—maybe even without lights, so as not to attract attention—fail to take this bend here, in an unfamiliar car, and go crashing over the edge. Possibly he'd be thrown out. At any rate, even if he stayed in until it reached the river, he'd be so dazed and knocked about that he might not be able to find the jewels, or even to think about them, then."

"Jove—you make it sound pretty convincing, Ian." Almost reluctantly, Don could not keep the admiration out of his voice. "And you think he might have known about Houndswyre Tower, and made his way there to lie up?"

"Not necessarily. He may have just seen it against the skyline, when he came staggering up here. There's a half-moon at nights, just now. Injured like that, any place would look like a refuge to him. So he goes to ground there. And is waiting for the hue and cry to die down—and for himself to be fit enough to make a bolt for it."

"And meantime, he can't find the jewels!"

"Yes. If they weren't very securely bunked away in the car, they could have got shaken out and scattered. The thing rolling over and over, the way it must have done. Maybe he's got some of them, now, but not all."

"You've certainly got it all worked out. But we can't be sure that it happened that way at all," Don pointed out.

"No. But it's a possibility, at least."

"What on earth do we do now, then?" For once, Don was not the leader.

"I don't know. I mean—what we can do eventually. Just now, I think we should just watch Mickey Pat. See what he does."

"Yes. But don't let him see us. If he knows that we've seen him back at the car, he'll realise that we're bound to be very suspicious. We don't want that, do we? He might bolt, or something. Go and hide somewhere else, anyway."

Crouching behind the wall, the boys waited and watched. Presently the Irishman crept with difficulty out of the open car window again, taking a long time about it. Then he lay resting beside the chassis for a while, before painfully getting to his feet. He picked up a bit of a branch that he used as a walking-stick, and very slowly and with much trouble began to climb the hill, limping heavily.

"He looks very depressed," Don whispered. "He's not found what he was looking for."

"I don't know how he's managing to drag himself up there like that. Considering the difficulty we had with him. The pain must be awful. In one way he's pretty brave," the soft-hearted Ian pointed out.

It took a long time for Mickey Pat to climb up the bank. Not only because he was forced to go so slowly, one halting step at a time. He was searching the ground all the way up; obviously he was coming up by the route that the car had taken in its headlong career. Every now and again he stopped, to poke about in the longer grass with his stick. Sometimes he sat down for a minute or two at a time, sweat streaming down his face. On these occasions he grubbed about in the grass and loose soil with his hands.

"Not much doubt that he's looking for something that may have got thrown out of the car. And something small!" Don commented. "I shouldn't wonder if you're not perfectly right about it all, Ian."

The brothers slipped back out of sight, as Mickey Pat at last neared the road. They hid behind a tree as the Irishman hobbled wearily across, went through the gate, and began to struggle off across the rough pasture beyond, climbing towards the tower on its ridge. Whatever he had done, they could not help feeling sorry for the man, he looked so desperately tired and suffering. They were strongly tempted to come out of hiding and give him a hand back to his cell. But they realised that that would be foolish—and almost certainly gain them no gratitude from Mickey Pat himself. They watched, until they saw him pause, leaning against the side of the castle doorway, then stumble inside.

They looked at each other.

"Well, we've got to decide what we do now," Don said. "Do we . . . do we go to the police?"

Ian bit his lip. "I don't think we should do that—not yet. Do you? I mean . . ." He left unsaid what he meant.

"I know," his brother nodded. "It seems a pretty rotten trick, after looking after him all this time, to go and bring the police down on him. Sort of betraying him. And yet, if he is a jewel robber, we *ought* to, I suppose."

"We don't know for sure, of course. It's all just supposition," Ian said.

"You didn't sound as though you thought there was much supposition about it, a little while ago!"

"I know. But—well, we *may* be wrong. And it seems awful just to hand him over to the police if it's something not very bad that he's done. If it *was* poaching. When he's in such pain, too. I don't know what we can do, really. It's a terribly difficult position."

"If only we could ask somebody's advice. I don't think Aunt Mary would be much good, somehow."

"No. Anyway, we promised not to tell anyone. And that goes for the police too, of course. We couldn't go to them without breaking our promise. Even if they would listen to us, anyway. They weren't very ready to pay attention to us, up in Inverness-shire that time."

"No. There's that, too. But we can't just do nothing, Ian. That would be quite wrong, surely? I think . . . I think we'll just have to tell him. Tell Mickey Pat what we suspect. And that we'll have to do something about it—unless he can prove that we're all wrong. Perhaps we could convince him to go to the police himself? To give himself up. Show him that it would be the best thing, really."

"Do you see him doing it?"

"No-o-o. But it would let us out of our promise, at least."

"He would do a bunk, then. Get away."

"I suppose so, yes. But that's not really our responsibility. Or is it?"

"Goodness knows. I wish . . . I wish we'd never got mixed up in this, Don."

"I know. But who wanted to go poking about Houndswyre Tower?"

"We can't go up and put it to him just now, can we? Sick with pain as he is."

"No. Anyway, the time must be getting on." Don looked at his watch. "Goodness—it's nearly one o'clock! We'll be late for lunch as it is. And we're going to Rulekirk directly afterwards. We'll have to rush. We've got to get back to the bikes, too, first. We'll not be back to Denholm for half an hour yet."

They began to run.

CHAPTER SIX

To Tell or Not To Tell?

THEIR Aunt Mary probably thought that her two nephews from Edinburgh were rather less interested in a country town market day than they ought to have been; for her, Rulekirk was more or less the centre of the universe. Possibly, also, she was somewhat disappointed that they did not appear to be more thrilled and appreciative over the exciting picture of gangsters, car-bandits, and motor-cycle police. She herself, certainly, couldn't have imagined anything more alarming, and would never have gone near a cinema showing such an entertainment had she not had the boys to keep amused. Yet they remained thoughtful, quiet, not to say distracted, throughout the whole day, and were only mildly polite about the picture, when discussing it that evening. They had rather a lot on their minds, in fact.

The film itself had all seemed distinctly unreal and something of an anti-climax to the boys, who were hardly to be blamed for feeling that their own close-at-hand excitements and problems rather put into the shade these imaginary American cops and robbers.

The trouble was that they could not explain this to their aunt. Something happened, however, not in the cinema itself but just outside, that did impress them quite a lot, and set them furiously to think, thus sending them back in the bus from Rulekirk to Denholm noticeably quiet.

They had been walking along the High Street, one on either side of their aunt, when the swing-doors of a public house burst open, just as they were opposite, and amidst a great deal of shouting about half a dozen men spilled out into the street, fighting violently. Staggering out into the roadway, they continued to battle, swiping and punching at each other, not with any great deal of accuracy or efficiency, but with plenty of noise and cursing. More respectable customers came hurrying out after them, most of them merely to watch, some few to cheer on the contestants, one or two to hurry off along the street in the direction of the police station behind the town hall—but none to interfere in the fisticuffs, probably wisely.

Aunt Mary, of course, had hurried herself and her nephews promptly from the scene, outraged, and declaring that she didn't know what Rulekirk, the Borders, and indeed the world in general, were coming to, making for the bus stop at the other end of the little town. But she did not get them off the scene before they had heard quite enough of the shouting and swearing to reveal to the least expert that the fighters consisted of three Irishmen and three foreigners of some sort. The rights and wrongs of the matter were, of course, far from apparent—but the strong Irish brogues and the broken English were unmistakable. The crowd that gathered quickly did not seem to be unduly upset or surprised about it all, declaring that it was just those Brackenhope hydro-scheme navvies letting themselves go again.

The MacDonald boys were much affected—but not, it is to be feared, like their aunt, because of the disgraceful scene. They now perceived that there might well be ways whereby one Irish labourer might have come by certain unfortunate injuries other than by either the attentions of bullying gamekeepers or the effects of a car accident.

The next morning, Saturday, they once again asked for another whole-day picnic lunch. Probably their aunt was quite relieved to see them go; no doubt she decided that they were a very energetic pair. They were off on their bicycles by ten o'clock, and headed straight down Teviotdale for Houndswyre.

Although half-expecting Mickey Pat to be absent again, quite likely down at the wrecked car, they found him in fact sitting just inside the tower doorway and peering out. He seemed actually quite relieved to see them, as though he had been looking out for them. But he appeared to be agitated, nevertheless. Before they even had time to ask him how he was this morning, he was challenging them.

"Were you after bringing me the paper and envelope

like I told you, now?" he demanded. "I've a message for you to take, boys. Important it is. I have to write it down on paper. Och, it's to a sort of friend of mine, see. So have you got the paper?"

"Yes, I've got it here," Ian said. "Actually, we did bring it yesterday, but quite forgot to give it you, with all that business at the car. We remembered it after we'd left you, and . . . and . . ."

"Let's see it here, then. I have a piece of pencil." The man took the paper and envelope, without a word of thanks. Indeed he frowned at them as they stood there. "Now—off with you while I'm writing my letter."

"But, look . . . Mickey Pat—we want to speak to you."

"We do, indeed," Don agreed.

"Och—plenty of time for speaking afterwards. Mercy upon us—d'you think I can be writing with the two of you staring at every word I spell?" The Irishman was gripping his small stub of pencil firmly, rather as though it was a tool with which he was going to attempt a difficult job of work. Presumably for him the writing of letters was not a task to be undertaken lightly. He waved the boys away with the other hand.

Shrugging, they strolled off and sat down on the warm grass some short distance off.

"He seems pretty excited about something," Ian commented. "I wonder why he's suddenly so anxious to write this letter. Which he doesn't want us to see. It didn't seem so very urgent before."

"It may be just that he doesn't want to have to answer our questions," Don suggested. "He's pretty cute, you know. Yesterday he put us off by seeming to be terribly ill and in pain. To-day he's too busy with this letter. He knows perfectly well that we're wondering about that car. And other things, too, of course."

"Yes. But if it was just that, he could have hidden himself somewhere, couldn't he? I mean, kept out of our way. He needn't have been here obviously waiting for us. If he'd kept out of sight he wouldn't have had to answer questions. No—I think this letter's important. To him, anyway. He's not tried to get in touch with anybody, until now. Not that we know of. And you heard—he said it was to a sort of friend. Not to a wife or mother or anybody like that. It looks as though it has suddenly become important for him to contact somebody, for some reason."

"Something to do with the car, you think? The jewels?"

"Maybe. I don't know."

"Anyway, we mustn't be put off about asking him questions. Not any more. And telling him of our suspicions. So that we can be free of our promise, if nothing else. Not to tell anybody, I mean. Obviously it's high time that we did tell somebody."

"Yes. But . . . it's not going to be very nice. And

they *are* only suspicions, mind. It *might* have been the result of some fight, like last night. He might have been just keeping out of the way of some gang of other navvies, after being beaten up. Hiding here. They're obviously a wild crowd. We don't even know that he's a hydro-worker, of course. He might be one of these field-workers. Irish potato-lifters. That sort of thing. He hasn't told us anything about himself, really."

"That's all very well. But we did agree that we must question him. Let him see that we're not just to be made fools of. Have our legs pulled, this way. We made up our minds . . ."

It was quite a while before Mickey Pat shouted to them that he was finished his writing. They were getting quite impatient. He had sealed up the letter in the envelope by the time that they came up—so there was no seeing what sort of an epistle it was. No address was written on the envelope, either.

"Here you are, then, boys," he said, holding it out.

"You take this to Stefan, see. Stefan Dubitsky. Up at the camp. Five bob for the pair of you for taking it, see."

"But . . . just a minute, Mickey Pat," Don said doubtfully. "I don't know if we can do this . . ."

"Och, of course you can. Why couldn't you, at all? It'll not be taking you an hour, on your bikes, to the camp. Six miles, maybe? Seven? Och, I'll make it five bob each—there you are. Ten bob for the job—easy money."

"It's not that," Ian told him. "We don't want your money, Mickey Pat. It's just that . . . well, we're not very happy about all this."

"There's nothing to it, boy, I'm telling you. Just you cycle up to Brackenhope Camp. The water scheme. There's a kind of hostel there—a big ould house. Ask the woman at the hostel for Stefan Dubitsky. It's a rum sort of a name, bedad—but och, he can't help it, the man. He's a Pole or a Ukrainian, or something. He's my mate, see. And you give him this letter. That's all."

"You do work at the new reservoir scheme, then," Don said, glancing at his brother. "At Brackenhope? Not, not . . . ?"

"Sure, I do. Me and Stefan work a concrete-mixer."

The twins exchanged glances. That disposed of the idea that it could have been an employer's car, anyway.

Ian took a long breath. "Mickey Pat," he said determinedly. "Where did you get that car down there? The wrecked car?"

Keenly the Irishman looked at him from bright blue eyes, in a moment's silence. "What you talking about, boy?" he jerked. "Faith—what nonsense is this you're at now?"

"That car." Doggedly Ian went on. "You knew that car was down there—or you'd never have walked all that way to it. Especially with your sore ankle. You'd never have gone all that way from the tower, on chance, with a bad leg and injured as you are. You knew it was there, and you were very interested in it, for some reason. You were looking for something inside it, I think. You were at it more than once, too."

"Yes—and you knew that there was no driver injured," Don put in, in support. "We believe that is because you were the driver yourself. That is how you got your injuries—crashing down that bank in the car. Not fighting with gamekeepers at all."

"It wasn't a fight—it was a massacre, bedad! Five to one, they were, the lousy limbs o' Satan . . .!"

"Four to one it was before! But that's not important," Ian went on. "If it was a fight, we're pretty sure that it was not keepers or bailiffs. Or that you were poaching at all. Not for salmon, at any rate. That's not a salmon river. Keepers and bailiffs wouldn't be watching it."

There was an uncomfortable silence.

Don spoke into it. "We think there's something very queer about the whole business," he said. "We want to know what it is, before we do anything more for you, Mickey Pat."

The man stroked his chin, red with three days' growth of beard, and looked from one to the other. "So you'd run out on me, would you, the pair of you? Murder alive—you'd try to do me dirt, so you would?"

"We haven't done you dirt so far, have we?" Don protested hotly. "We've done a lot for you. We've done all you've asked—more than we should, I think. Any dirt that's been done—you've done it, I think!"

"You've not been honest with us, that's obvious," Ian added.

The other took a long breath, and quite suddenly changed his tune. "Och, yes—you've been good boys. Sure and that's a fact. Look, lads—you are right, in a kind of way. I was driving that car, see. We were poaching, like I said. This Stefan and me. After we'd had our fight with the keepers and we got away from them, we got back to the car. Och, I was sort of dazed with the battering they gave me, the divvils, and I wasn't driving none too good, see. Upon my soul, as I was going round that bend in the road there, darned if the ould car didn't take the bit in its teeth bedad, and go lepping clean over the bank like a steeplechaser. Wow—but I thought Mickey Pat was dead and buried, that time, I tell you!"

"It must have been awful, yes. But . . ."

The twins were eyeing each other again, wondering how much to believe this time.

"If you'd told us this before . . ." Don began.

"The car," Ian interrupted. "It's a big one. And very expensive. A Humber. If you could afford that kind of car, Mickey Pat, you wouldn't need to poach your salmon! Or whatever it was you were poaching, for we don't believe it was salmon. Whose car is it?"

The man hesitated only for a moment. "Faith, it's not my car, no. It's a friend of Stefan's that belongs to it. Wasn't he just borrowing it for the night."

"A fine big expensive shooting-brake like that? Just to go on a poaching expedition?" Don shook his head. "I don't think that we can believe that, Mickey Pat. And . . . you don't mind us mentioning it, do you?—but would your friend Stefan, working a concrete mixer, be likely to have the sort of friend who would own a car like that? We . . . we rather think, in fact, that it is a stolen car!"

"You do, do you? You nasty suspicious little divvils! So you reckon I'd do a thing the like of that? Steal a car!"

"Actually . . . h'rr'mm . . . we rather wondered whether you hadn't been stealing something else as well! Jewels, for instance!"

It took Mickey Pat a few moments to find his protesting breath. "Jewels, is it? Suffering saints alive!—jewels, now! First a car, and now jewels, bedad! Is that what you think of me?" The injured man shook his red head reproachfully, sadly.

"Well—there was a big jewel robbery that same night, and not far from here," Ian pointed out. "And we know that the Swale Water isn't a salmon river at all. So, you see . . ."

"Is that so? Och, and I daresay there was a couple of men murdered dead, some place, a racehorse doped likely, and . . . and ould Mother Riley's chicken-roost raided into the bargain, all the self-same night! But you'll not be holding Mickey Pat responsible for them all, by Glory!"

"No-o-o. But you must admit it's suspicious. What *were* you doing—for it wasn't really salmon, was it?"

"Och, well . . ." The man shrugged. "No, it wasn't salmon, to be sure. It was game. Pheasants, see you. We were after the pheasants, that's what it was."

"Why did you tell us salmon, then?"

"Och, what's the difference, pheasants or salmon? I . . . well, I reckoned that salmon sounded sort of better, see. It was pheasants I was pinched for the other time . . ."

"It wasn't pheasants that you were looking for in that car, was it? Something a bit smaller, I think!" Ian said. "You were looking for something, weren't you? You can't deny it. We saw you."

"Sure I was. I had a wrist-watch that my poor ould father gave me, years and years ago—may he rest in peace! It came off me, some way, in the crash. The strap must have broke, for sure. I've been trying to find it. I reckoned it must be in the car still—though, och, it might just have fallen out on the bank, at that."

Ian frowned. "Oh," he said, not knowing what else to say.

Don tried to be more tough. "That may be so, Mickey Pat—but you've not been telling us the truth, at all, have you? Before. So we just can't believe you. Everything's different from what you said. How can you expect us to believe this, about the watch?"

"Believe it or not—please yourselves."

"No—but because we can't believe you, any more, we can't promise you any more either that we won't tell anybody else about you . . ."

"Divvil—you haven't gone and told anyone, have you, boy? Not yet?" That was quick.

"No. We promised. We haven't told a soul. But we're not promising any more, Mickey Pat."

The man's sudden intense anxiety had been as obvious as was his sudden relief now. But he sighed and shook his head, just the same. "So you've finished with poor Mickey Pat, have you? You'll be doing no more for me? You won't help me—and you won't take my message for Stefan to help me either! Och, it's a bad business for a man sick and ill like I am . . ."

"We didn't say we'd not do any more for you," Ian told him. "If you'll tell us the truth—if you'll give us your word of honour that it wasn't you who stole the jewels . . ."

"Och, and I'll do that, boy—sure and I will! Right now I will. Cross my heart and soul—I never stole a jewel in all my born days, and that's a fact. Nor ever will." That came out with a rush.

The brothers looked from the Irishman to each other perplexedly. They could hardly just say again that they did not believe this either. It was all very difficult.

"Well . . ." Don said uncertainly. "If you're sure."

"You'll help me then, boys? You'll still help me? You'll be taking my letter to Stefan? Och, the saints bless and preserve the pair of you! Fine lads you are. Bedad, yes!" Mickey Pat grinned hugely, actually thrust out a grimy hand and insisted in shaking hands with them both. "That's fine, then. Never another thing more will I ask of you, to be sure."

"But, look . . ." Ian objected. "We're not quite satisfied yet, you know. I mean, you haven't told us what it's all about, even yet. All we know is that you didn't take the jewels."

"Och, you know it all now, to be sure. About the pheasants, and Stefan's friend's car. D'you want me to go down on my bended knees and swear a holy oath, that I've told you everything that ever happened to me in all my life?"

"No, no—nothing like that, of course. We're just . . . well, not wholly satisfied yet. That's all."

"Och, well—who is, at all? I'm not, bedad! But you've said you'll take my letter for me, haven't you now? You'll not be going back on that? It's the last thing I'll ever ask of you, and that's a fact."

Somehow the twins found it quite impossible either to refuse to take the message, or to go on asserting to Mickey Pat's face that they did not believe him. In fact, all that they really wanted, at the moment, was to get away from the Irishman before he involved them in anything else. Somehow or other they felt embarrassed and uncomfortable. And since he was urging them to be off, not to waste any time, that the letter was urgent, and so on, they found themselves taking leave of him. At least, however, they firmly refused the ten shillings that the Irishman offered them, and hurried off with the letter. Shouted blessings followed them down the side of the ridge.

Out of earshot, Ian shook his head helplessly. "I must say, I don't like this, Don," he said. "We didn't make a good job of that, at all. We've just sort of foozled it, haven't we? I mean, we probably shouldn't be doing this at all. Taking this message. But . . ."

"I know. But what else *could* we have done? I don't really trust him. Do you? Do you believe him, about the jewels? And the car? And the pheasants?"

"No, I don't. At least—maybe about the jewels. He seemed definite enough about that. But about the other things—I just don't know what to make of him. For there's . . . there's something rather nice about him, too, you know. When he smiles. I can't feel that he's really bad. Can you? Obviously he's got into a real packet of trouble, and I should think that he quite often does things that he ought not to do! But so do we all, don't we? It's a matter of degree, I suppose." Ian sighed. "Anyway, we couldn't just refuse to take a letter for him, could we? When it was obviously important for him. Especially when he swore that he hadn't taken the jewels—whatever else he's been up to. Maybe we're misjudging him? Being too clever? And at least he didn't try to make us promise not to tell anybody, again. I was afraid of that. We're free of that promise now, at any rate."

"Yes, I know. That was one of the reasons why I wanted to get away from him quickly, just now. In case he thought of that—asked us again not to tell. It's a comfort to know that, since we've told him that the promise doesn't stand any more, we *can* ask advice about what's best. I must admit, I could do with some really sensible advice from somebody about what to do with Mickey Pat!"

"You're telling me! But, you know—if we can sort of turn him over to this friend of his, Stefan What's-his-name, then that more or less lets us out, doesn't it? He's *his* friend, and can look after him. We'll tell him where Mickey Pat is hiding, and then it's not really up to us to do anything more about him, is it?"

"M'mmm. That's true. Only—you mean that we shouldn't tell the police, at all? About the car, or anything?"

"I . . . I don't know. I just don't know. Perhaps we might think of somebody to tell—not the police, necessarily. More to ask advice. Then . . ."

"Yes. That will be the best thing. We might go to Doctor Mackay, at Denholm. He's a nice man, and would probably tell us what we should do. To-night, eh?"

Glad to have reached a decision at last, the boys mounted their bicycles and set off on their long run to Brackenhope—more like ten miles than Mickey Pat's six or seven.

CHAPTER SEVEN

Bird Flown

Brackenhope lay high up amongst the big hills, to the west of Teviotdale. It took a lot of hard pedalling, and much pushing of bikes, to get there. It would be much better coming back, the boys told each other. Quite a large valley was to be flooded, to make a reservoir for some of the Border towns, and a great dam was being built across the foot of it. As they neared the scheme, they found the entire area in a terrible mess, the ground churned up by heavy vehicles, dumps, pipes and rusting machinery scattered around, and mud everywhere. Ian saw it as a perfectly good piece of country absolutely ruined; but Don said that it represented progress, man's triumph over the forces of nature, and all most interesting and exciting.

Asking some men who were climbing into a lorry where the hostel was, the boys were directed to a large, gaunt and bare building that was the former mansion house of Brackenhope, all its fine trees cut down and its shrubberies flattened, its windows without curtains and some of them broken, amid a general air of neglect. They pulled at a big, old-fashioned bell at the pillared front door, but this did not seem to ring, and certainly nobody came. After knocking a number of times without result, they ventured inside.

What had once been an imposing hall was utterly empty save for a handsome marble mantelpiece, now broken, above a choked-up fireplace. Though they rapped on various doors, and eventually shouted for attention, nothing happened. But the place was not quite deserted, for they could hear rough voices from somewhere upstairs.

They were about to venture up there when Don, sniffing, said that he could smell cooking coming from the back premises. Following their noses along passages and around corners, they at last came to what presumably was the kitchen of the hostel, where a woman and a girl worked at large stove and sinks.

Don was the spokesman, knocking at the open door. "I say—is this the hostel, please? For Brakenhope workers. Could you tell us?"

The woman, middle-aged and pleasant enough, nodded. "Aye, it is, laddie. What can I do for you?"

"You are the . . . well, the lady in charge? We were to ask you to guide us to a man called Stefan. Stefan Du . . . Du . . ."

"Dubitsky," Ian prompted. "Is he here?"

"Stefan? Och, he was, aye. Stefan Dubitsky, that's right."

"Do you think that we could see him, please? We have a message for him."

"Dearie me, I doubt you'll no' see Stefan, laddies," the woman said, shaking her head. "He's gone."

"Gone?"

"Aye. He's gone, the man. No' that long since, either."

"What d'you mean—gone? You mean he's left here?"

"That's right. He was here till this morning, just. But this is Saturday, see. And now he's gone."

"You mean, for the week-end?" Ian asked. "He'll be back on Monday?"

"No, he'll no' be back at all, lad. I tell you, he's gone. Away to England some place, I think. Aye, Manchester, it was."

"But . . . but . . ."

"Och, if you'd come an hour or so earlier you'd have got him. He got a lift down on a truck an hour back, just. He's no' been well, this week. Off his work. He had some sort o' an accident at the beginning o' the week. Now he's taken his books and gone . . ."

"An accident! At the beginning of the week?" Don interrupted. "Could that have been on Tuesday night?"

"Tuesday? Aye, I dare say it was about then, lad. They're aye having accidents these fellows. Right careless they are. It seems to be a dangerous game, building a dam."

Don and Ian nodded to each other.

"Are you sure that he's gone? For good, I mean?" Ian asked.

"Oh, aye. He's packed his bag and away. Said he'd had enough of this job. He said he knew of a job he could get down Manchester way. He's catching the one-fifteen train from Rulekirk. That'll be to Carlisle. Isn't that what he said, Jeannie?"

"Aye," the girl agreed. "It's the only one there is, to the south anyway, till night time. Right sudden he was about it."

"Aye. It was the accident seemed to upset him. He was a queer-like man, anyway. Did you know him, you two?"

"Er . . . no. We just have a message for him. From a . . . a friend." Don was looking at his watch. "It's twelve-thirty now. How far it it to Rulekirk from here?"

"Och, it's the best part of four miles. Aye, it'll be all of that. Are you thinking you could catch him, maybe?"

"We might. If we hurried. We've got bikes. And it's downhill most of the way."

"Och, you'd never do it on bikes," the woman said. "Is it all that important?"

"I . . . we don't quite know. But it may be."

"Yes, it may be. I think, you know, we should hurry. Thank you—thank you very much."

"Dinna thank me. If you ask me, laddies, yon Stefan's no' worth the hurrying after! I never much liked the look of him, and that's a fact."

"Oh. Well—good-bye."

"Er . . . was he much of a fisherman, by the way? This Stefan?" Ian asked. "Or a shooter? Pheasants?"

"Fisherman? Him! Och, I wouldna think he'd ken one end of a fish from the other. Or a pheasant. Why?"

"Oh, nothing. Nothing. Well—thanks again."

Outside, the twins put their heads together—but not for long.

"He had an accident too—and at the same time," Ian said. "But he got back here, all right. Alone. What do'you think that means?"

"Goodness knows—except that he can't have been as badly hurt as Mickey Pat."

"No. And now he's doing a bunk. To England. Not coming back. It doesn't look as though he's very worried about his friend! And he doesn't seem to have been much of a poacher! I wonder . . . ?"

"What are you getting at, Ian?"

"I'm just wondering if this Stefan hasn't got the jewels!"

"My goodness! You think he's maybe running off with them?"

"Look—the poaching story seems to be a fake from start to finish. Yet the two of them were doing something with that big expensive car, quite near where the robbery was. Suppose this Stefan was the jewel thief, and our Mickey Pat just the driver of the getaway car?"

"Yes. Yes—it could be that. Then, I suppose,

Mickey Pat *could* swear, in a kind of way, that he'd never stolen a jewel in his life!"

"There was a crash—but Stefan wasn't so badly hurt as his friend. Perhaps he came back to the wrecked car, later. That night or the next day. Took the jewels. That would account for Mickey Pat not being able to find what he was looking for."

"Of course. That's right. And I've just thought of something else, Ian. Remember how Mickey Pat wanted that newspaper? Not the one we brought him, on the Thursday. But the day before's. He may have been wanting to read about the robbery, and whether his missing friend had been caught!"

"Yes. That could be it. I say—it all fits in, doesn't it? I wonder . . . I wonder what's in that envelope? What Mickey Pat says to him?"

"D'you think we should open it? Now?"

"We can hardly do that. Just on supposition. We might take it to the police, though. So that they could stop this Stefan getting away, if it's what we think."

"But that would take ages. Explaining everything to them. You know how unbelieving the police can be, when it's just boys like ourselves telling them something. Stefan could be most of the way to Carlisle before we'd convinced them that we weren't making the whole thing up."

"That's true. Yes, the main thing, the first thing, is to stop Stefan getting away on that train, if we can. Otherwise he can just disappear. If we got Mickey

Pat's letter to him, and told him where he was hiding, he would probably wait and go there. To see him. He won't know what on earth's happened to his friend."

"Quick, then—we'll have to fly. Absolutely. We've less than forty minutes."

The boys had been pushing their bicycles as they talked. Now they jumped up into their saddles, and started to pedal faster than they had ever done in their lives before.

At first, by muddy churned-up roads, despite all their efforts, their progress was maddeningly slow. Fretting, more than once they had to dismount and lift their bikes over bad patches. But as they won clear of the construction area, road conditions began to improve, and presently they were free-wheeling at a crazy pace down the long hills towards the Teviot valley. There were sudden steep slopes in the other direction, too, of course, that held them up; but most of the time they were descending. They were very lucky not to have any spills, for they took some of their corners much faster than was wise.

Don kept taking his eyes off the road, too, to glance at his watch.

At last they saw the grey roofs and mill chimneys of Rulekirk in the valley below them, still some distance off but at least not now seeming impossibly out of reach.

"We've exactly eight minutes left," Don shouted. "Will we do it?"

"Don't know," Ian yelled back. "Maybe the train will be late. They often are, a bit."

Six minutes later they flung their bicycles against the Rulekirk Station railings, and went racing up the steps to the platform, high above the river, gasping for breath.

On the platform six people were waiting; three were women, one was a soldier, and the fifth was very obviously a businessman in black coat and bowler hat. The sixth was a dark, sallow, youngish man with long sideburns, dressed in an ex-Army jerkin, stained corduroys and hob-nailed boots. He carried a cheap suitcase.

"Bound to be him," Don panted. "Come on."

"Tickets, please," the collector at the gate demanded.

"Oh, goodness!" Ian cried. "We aren't going on the train. We haven't tickets. We've got to see one of those people. It's important."

"You'd better get a platform ticket, then," the man said.

"We haven't time . . ."

"Look," Don thrust his hand into his trousers pocket and drew out a sixpence. "You buy them for us. Please."

Without waiting for agreement, they rushed past the collector on to the platform.

CHAPTER EIGHT

A Quick Decision

A GLANCE along the line showed that the train was signalled. The boys hurried up to the dark, sallow young man.

"I say," Don panted. "Are you Stefan? Stefan Du . . . Dubitsky? From the Brackenhope camp?"

The man frowned. He did not look at all pleased to see them. He was quite good-looking in a flashy sort of way, but thin-lipped, piercing-eyed, tough.

"What you want?" he jerked.

"You *are* Mr. Dubitsky?" Ian insisted. "We've rushed down from the camp, to catch you. Before the train came." He looked hurriedly along the line again. "We have a letter for you." He pulled the crumpled envelope out of his pocket.

The man looked almost as though he did not want to take the letter, did not want to have anything to do with them. "Who are you boys?" he demanded.

"Our name is MacDonald. But that's not important. Look—please read this letter. Quickly. There isn't much time before the train comes. It's from your friend. From Mickey Pat."

The other's dark eyes widened now. Then his frown

came down blacker than ever. He snatched the envelope from Ian's hand, and turning his back on them paced a couple of steps away, to open and read the letter.

In the distance, the boys could hear the thin, high whistle of the oncoming train echoing amongst the green hills.

It didn't seem to be a long letter, or take a lot of reading at any rate, for after only a moment or two the man thrust it into his pocket, and turned back to them.

"Okay," he said. That was all.

The boys waited for a few seconds. Then they stared from him to each other, as it dawned upon them that this was apparently all that Stefan Dubitsky had to say to them.

"But . . . I say! The letter?" Don exclaimed. "What . . . what . . . ?" He could hardly demand to know what it said.

"What about Mickey Pat?" Ian said.

The man did not answer. Did not even look at them.

"Listen!" Don went on urgently. "You've got to listen. The train will be here any minute now. Mickey Pat's had an accident. You know that. But he's injured. We can take you to him. We've been looking after him."

"Scram!" Stefan Dubitsky said shortly.

"But . . . but this is daft! You are his friend, his mate. He told us. He needs help. He's got a bad ankle.

If you'd come with us, we'd take you to where he is hiding."

"That letter—he was very anxious that you should get it. Mickey Pat was. He offered us ten shillings to get it to you. He must have expected you to do *something* about it," Ian pointed out.

The other began to walk away from them, along the platform.

"Hang it all, you can't do this!" Don protested, hurrying after him. "We've gone to a lot of trouble. Mickey Pat needs you. Come and see him. Please. You can get the next train . . ."

Dubitsky turned on him, almost with a snarl. "Go away!" he snapped. "You boys, you talk too much. Go away! Scram!" And he raised a hand in a threatening gesture.

Two women waiting nearby looked at them all very curiously.

The rumble of the approaching train itself could now be heard, perfectly clearly.

Helplessly the twins drew back. They could not *force* the man to listen to them, to do anything.

"The brute!" Don burst out angrily. "The rotten, callous brute!"

"What can we do? We can't stop him."

"He shouldn't be allowed to get away with this. Obviously he doesn't care a hoot for his friend."

"He doesn't care to share the loot with him, you mean!" Ian said. "I'm jolly sure that's what it is. He's got the jewels out of the car, and now all he wants is to get away with them. For himself. He's probably got the necklace and the rest on him now."

"Goodness—that's right. That'll be it. Ian—we've got to do something to stop him. We've got to."

"But, what? The police . . . ?"

"Listen! Once he gets away on that train, he's gone. And the jewels, too. Nobody will be able to trace him. He'll disappear into some big English city, and that will be the end of it."

"If only we'd gone to the police first."

"We hadn't time. We'd never have managed to explain it all in time. Gosh—here's the train now. I can see its smoke. Look, Ian—I'm going on that train, too! To keep an eye on this man—keep in touch with him . . ."

"But, Don—you can't do that!"

"I can. You go to the police. Tell them everything. Tell them that I'm on the train, too, watching him. They could arrange for it to be stopped. By telephone."

"But . . . but if they don't believe me?" Ian almost wailed.

"You've got to make them believe you. Somehow."

"You've no money. For the ticket . . ."

"Never mind that. The main thing is not to let this Stefan out of our sight. Or my sight, anyway. Here it is—the train. Look—we'll walk away. Inside the booking-hall place. As though we were leaving. So that he doesn't suspect anything. Then, when I see what compartment he gets into, I'll nip out and into the train, just as it's starting. So that that collector man can't stop me. It's sure to be a corridor train—long-distance ones always are. I'll go and sit in the next compartment, so that I can keep a watch on him. Okay?"

When it came to action, rather than reasoning, Don always took the lead.

Ian shook his head. "I don't really think you should do this, Don. Everything may go wrong. You may get carried away goodness knows where. And that horrible man might get nasty. If he sees you. You may get into all sorts of trouble."

"Not if you do your stuff with the police. Only—you'll have to be quick about it. I say, you'll have to be quick . . ."

His voice was drowned in the thunderous noise of the train as it came clanking in to the platform amidst a hissing of steam and a screeching of brakes.

Very few people got out. They watched Stefan Dubitsky, after a quick look round, get into a second-class compartment well back on the train, slamming the door behind him.

Don waited until the last passenger had climbed aboard, and down at the end of the platform the guard stepped out, blew his whistle and waved his green flag. Then, giving a last firm clutch to his brother's arm, Don darted forward, and as the train slowly began to move, flung open the end door of a carriage and jumped up. He turned to give a brief wave as he pulled the door shut behind him.

Ian stared after the train, biting his lip, in something that wasn't very far from panic.

At the gate, after the few passengers had passed through, Ian could delay no longer. The collector looked at him, frowning.

"Say, you—where's your pal?" he demanded. "There were two of you."

"I'm afraid . . . well, he decided to take the train. At the last moment. We didn't mean to do that—I mean, before." Ian floundered. "It . . . it suddenly became necessary, you see."

"It did, did it? Necessary, eh, my young cockerel? And so's a ticket necessary when you travel on British Railways. Nobody ever tell you that, eh?"

"Oh, yes. But this was different. A special occasion . . ."

"Sure it's a special occasion. Jings, it is! And you'll just come right along with me to see the stationmaster, m'lad." An authoritative hand descended on Ian's shoulder. "It's an offence, see, to travel on a train without a ticket."

"No—please! Not just now. Do let me past. It's terribly important. Really."

"Sure it's important. That's why we're going to see the stationmaster."

"No, no. I just haven't time just now. Really—that's

the truth. Look—I'll come back and explain everything later. Honestly."

"You'll do your explaining now, young feller—not later. Come on, now."

"Please. It's the police I've got to go to. You must believe me. There was a man on that train that the police want. We were following him. My brother decided the only thing to do was to keep him in sight. So he got on the train, too. And I'm going to the police."

"A likely story! Jings—as good as the pictures! Na, na—you'll come with me."

"Listen—*you* take me to the police station, if you don't believe me. I'm going there, anyway. Only, hurry. For every moment is important. To my brother."

"Sakes—d'you think I've time to go traipsing down to the other side o' the town, to the police station? My job's here. The stationmaster will see to you, young man . . ."

Ian gulped a deep breath, ducked suddenly and twisted round—and his shoulder was free. Without waiting for another moment he dashed out through the gate and down the steps beyond, three at a time, almost toppling headlong in his haste.

At the foot he looked back. The collector was coming down after him, shouting angrily and shaking a fist. But he was an elderly man, and no match for Ian in a hurry.

"Sorry!" he called back. "It's just that there's no time. Not now. Lots depends on me. Phone the police if you like. I'll be there."

He grabbed up his bicycle, leaving Don's where it was, and jumping on, started to pedal furiously for the bridge over the Teviot and into the town. He did not know where the police station was, but somebody would tell him.

CHAPTER NINE

Telling the Police

Breathlessly, Ian ran into the public office of the police station, behind the Town Hall, and up to the public counter. A large lady was there, telling a burly young constable the full details of the life and times of her poodle dog, which apparently was missing. The policeman had already many lines of notes in his note-book on the subject, and was obviously going to have a lot more.

Ian waited, nibbling his lips with impatience. The lady's voice droned on and on. Another policeman glanced in, from a door at the back, saw what was going on, and hastily disappeared again just as Ian raised an urgent hand to attract his attention.

At last, when the sighing constable was hearing about what the poodle's grand-sire had done in the way of prize-winning long years before, Ian could stand it no longer.

"I say!" he broke in desperately. "I'm sorry to interrupt. But it's terribly important. Really. I'm in an awful hurry. Could somebody attend to me, please?"

The lady turned on him with an astonished frown. "Well—I must say!" she objected. "How rude can these modern children get? This is an impertinence."

The constable, however, looked almost relieved. "Ah, ummm," he said. "Is your house on fire, or something, laddie?"

"No—it's not that. But it's something very serious. And important. And there's not much time . . ."

"Be quiet, boy!" the lady commanded. "Wait your turn, like other people have to do. You are not the only one to whom time is important. Now, Constable—I want you to take careful note that Zazu is a highly nervous and sensitive creature. When she is found, I want her kept exactly where she is, until I come for her in my car. You understand? And no feeding her with what may well be highly unsuitable food. She is probably suffering agonies at the present moment, poor dear. Some horrible person has likely got hold of her. So . . ."

Ian groaned. "Look—I *must* see somebody. At once. I simply must. Every minute counts."

"Be quiet, child!"

"Just bide a wee minute, sonny. I'll no' be long. I hope."

"No. Sorry. I want to see the inspector. Now."

"Well—of all the impudence! Constable—this boy should be taught a lesson. I've never heard the like of it. And in a police station, too!"

"The inspector's out, lad. But if you'll just have a

wee bit patience. We all have to have patience, now and then, you know!"

"But, listen—my brother's being carried away to Carlisle. On the train. With a jewel thief."

"Gracious me—the boy's mad, Constable! Stark, raving mad! You'll have to do something about him, you will indeed. But after you've attended to me, please. Now . . ."

Unhappily the policeman looked from one caller to the other, scratching his head with his pencil.

Ian could bear it no longer. There was a sort of gate in the public counter, with a hinged flap above it. Throwing this up and the gate open, he darted through, running across the office and heading for the door to the inner quarters behind. The constable's voice was raised behind him—but not nearly so high as was the lady's.

Slipping through the inner door, Ian found himself in a corridor that ran left and right. On impulse he turned right—and ran smack into the arms of a large and solid blue-uniformed figure.

"Well, now—what's this? What's all this about, young man? You going somewhere?" a deep voice demanded.

Ian saw the three white chevrons of a sergeant quite close to his nose. "Oh, thank goodness!" he exclaimed. "Please—I want to speak to you."

"You do, do you? You seem very keen about it, I must say . . ."

"Sorry, Sarge." The constable appeared in the doorway from the office. "He nipped in through the office. He's been talking a bit wild, the boy. I was busy. With Mrs. Ochterlonie. You, h'm, know Mrs. Ochterlonie!"

"Aye," the sergeant said heavily, still holding on to Ian. "This boy's not with her, is he?"

"Och, no. It's about that, that dog again. Zazu. Aye, Zazu. I . . ."

"Please, Sergeant," Ian pleaded.

"All right, Willie. Well, young man—what have you to say for yourself?"

"It's very important. My brother Don—he's on this train, going to England. He hasn't a ticket. Did the stationmaster not phone you? He's following a man. Called Stefan Dubitsky. We think that he's a jewel thief."

"Mercy on us! Now, now, boy—one thing at a time. You're telling me that your brother's travelling on a train without a ticket? That it?"

"Yes, yes. But that's not the important thing. It's this man . . ."

"It's important enough, my lad. Do you mean that he went on to the train deliberately without paying his fare? Or that he was just sort of carried away by accident, when the train started?"

"No, no—he went deliberately. But that's really nothing to do with it, sir. I mean—you must listen to the important part. It's this man Dubitsky. Stefan Dubitsky . . ."

"How d'you spell it?" The sergeant enquired.

"Oh, D-U-B-I-T-S-K-Y. Please, don't start writing it down. Not just now. Time is everything—can't you see? With the train getting farther and farther away."

"All right, then. But, mind—you'd better not be pulling my leg, boy. Or you'll be sorry. What about this Du-What's-It?"

"We believe that he is the man who stole the countess's jewels. You know—the Countess of, of . . . oh, I've forgotten where. But it was last Tuesday night. At Swaleholm House. The necklace worth £20,000."

"Is that a fact? Just like that. You believe it, do you?"

"Yes, we do. We might be wrong, but I don't think so."

"I'm glad to hear that you think there may be a possibility of your being wrong," the sergeant mentioned, with heavy sarcasm. "We can all make mistakes, can't we!"

"Yes. I mean—I don't think we've made a mistake this time. The man's running away, now. He's on this train. The one that's just left the station. Don went along, too, to keep an eye on him. In the next compartment."

"Uh-huh. Without a ticket?"

"Yes. It was the only thing that we could do. While I came here, to you."

"You could have come here in the first place, could

you not? If you believed it was all that important?"

"We had no time. We came racing down from Brackenhope on our bikes. He'd left there about an hour before, to catch this train. If we'd come here first we'd have missed him. But, please—can we not talk about all this later? Can you not stop the train, now? By telephone?"

"Stop the train? Heavens, boy—you did say *stop* the train?"

"Yes. Telephone the signal people or something. That would stop it. Or have it held up at one of the stations down the line."

"Well, well! Look, young man—who d'you think I am? I'm just an ordinary sergeant o' police."

"Well," Ian said, politely but firmly, "if you can't do it, will you please take me to somebody who can?"

The other drew a long breath. "Laddie," he said, after a moment or two. "The trouble with you is you've been looking at the television. That's what it is!"

"No. It's nothing of the sort. We don't have television. But . . . this is awful! Surely there must be some way of getting something done? We're sure this man is the jewel robber. It's obvious, really."

"Obvious, is it? See here, now—I'm trying to be patient with you, boy. The police forces of both kingdoms have been looking for the character who did this Swaleholm job for days. Without a trace. Except that there's a slim lead that he may have got across to the Continent. And now you come barging in here to say you've picked him up. Just like that. Easy! Obvious, you say!"

"Well, it's true. We found a man hiding in Houndswyre Tower. Injured. He said he'd been poaching and had a fight with keepers. The same night as the robbery. We believed it, at first. But then we found him hunting about in a wrecked car. When he said he couldn't walk. Obviously looking for something. We think it was the jewels. He wouldn't admit it, of course. Then he gave us a letter to take to this Stefan Dubitsky. At Brackenhope Camp. When we got there, we found that he'd just packed up and gone. To-day. To catch this train. So we came racing after him . . ."

"My goodness—and you mean to tell me that, just because of this rigmarole, you've decided he's a jewel thief? It's worse than the TV you've been at—it's the horror comics!"

"But it's true. All of it. You must believe me. It's serious . . ."

"What's serious, young feller, is that your brother is on that train without authority and without a ticket. Possibly pestering a passenger. I'd better have your parents' name and address. Then we'll see what we can do about getting him safely collected. But you'll both be sorry for this nonsense. I'm warning you."

"No, no, no!" Ian cried. He looked round about him,

desperately, the sergeant still clutching his shoulder. The constable from the public office had presumably got rid of Mrs. Ochterlonie at last, and was now watching interestedly from the doorway.

"D'you want me to take down the particulars, Sarge?" he asked helpfully.

"Aye. You'd better, Willie. I'm busy just now. And watch this youngster. Don't let him get away, mind . . ."

"I'm not trying to get away! How can I convince you that it's all true?" Ian demanded, trying hard to control his voice. "I tell you, we saw him twice—this other man—searching the wrecked Humber. Down in the Swale Water. It was difficult for him to get into, because it was upside down. And he was injured. But he got in through a broken window—it was one of those shooting-brake things. And he he was searching the upholstery. For something small . . ."

"Sure, sure. But I haven't time for the whole serial story now, see."

"Sarge," the constable interrupted. "D'you hear that? He said a Humber. A Humber shooting-brake. There's one o' them on the new list o' stolen cars. A Super Snipe. What colour was it, laddie?"

"It was dark red. We should have taken the number, I suppose, but we forgot."

"That's right, Sarge. A maroon Humber Super Snipe station wagon, it says. Belonging to Colonel Kerr,

Saughtree House. Stolen the same night as the robbery."

"H'mmm," the sergeant said. "Er . . . indeed. Well, now."

"I *told* you . . ."

"Where d'you say this car is, boy?"

"In the Swale Water. Upside down. At the foot of a steep bank near Houndswyre Tower. And this man, Stefan Dubitsky, was in it at the time of the accident, on Tuesday night. The other man admitted that. He was slightly hurt, too. He's been off his work at Brackenhope all week, but he's fit enough to travel now. And he's off to England on this train—left his job. And not caring about his friend. The one at the Tower."

The two policemen exchanged glances.

"Maybe, Sarge . . . ?" the constable suggested.

"Aye, Willie—maybe. I think—aye, I think we might go upstairs and see the super."

"Oh, quick then!" Ian urged. "We've wasted absolute ages already. The super? Is that superintendent? Is he higher than the inspector?"

"Aye—he's the boss. So you'd better be careful what you say, boy. I hope you're no' talking a lot of nonsense, mind. . . "

CHAPTER TEN

Action!

The superintendent, a crisp, iron-grey, middle-aged man, with a short, military moustache, was a different proposition, from the first. He treated Ian as a responsible person, and the whole subject in a business-like fashion. The fact, of course, that the matter had been thought important enough to bring before himself, undoubtedly would help. He listened to the sergeant's stolid report, and Ian's excited interruptions, from behind a big desk, putting in a brief and pointed question here and there.

"Very good," he announced suddenly, cutting the sergeant short. "That's enough for the moment. This Dubitsky may not be the man we want, but at least we have to investigate him. Sergeant—have the booking office at the station phoned. Ask the clerk to where a man answering this description booked a ticket. Were there many passengers joining that train, young man?"

"No, sir. Three women, a soldier, a man in a bowler hat, and Dubitsky."

The superintendent permitted himself a faint smile. "Hear that, Sergeant? That's the sort of answer I like to a question. The clerk should be able to remember him easily, then. And I want to know what stops that train makes between here and Carlisle, and when." He glanced at his watch. "It has been gone over twenty minutes. But it's a long pull up to the summit, and they usually take on more water at Riccarton Junction. Quickly, now."

"Yessir."

"And Sergeant—send in my driver. At once."

Ian could not contain his relief. "Oh, I'm thankful I've found someone with some sense, at last!" he burst out. And then, flushing. "Oh, I'm sorry, sir."

The superintendent cocked one bristling eyebrow at him. "Don't crow too son, my young cockerel!" he advised. "There's many a slip, you know. And one can go too fast, as well as too slow. Remember that."

"Yes—but when you're racing a train, sir . . ."

The other nodded. "Quite," he said. He looked up. "Did this other man, the Irishman, say anything at all to make you suspect that he was mixed up in the jewel robbery?"

"No, not really, sir. He said, all the time, that he'd been poaching. But the Swale Water doesn't seem to be worth real poaching—for salmon. Or to have keepers on it. And he did want to see a newspaper. The paper of the day after the robbery. We brought him the wrong one, the next day's again, and he was quite annoyed. We think that he wanted to read about whether his friend Dubitsky had been captured, and what was happening."

"M'mmm. Well, it's a possible pointer—no more. Still, that car, the red Humber brake, was stolen from outside Swaleholm House, where Colonel Kerr was attending the Countess's party. The night that the jewels were stolen. One more pointer. And since they both point in the same direction . . ."

A knock at the door ushered in another constable.

"Macphail—I want my car available. At once. And have Number Four Patrol Car, and squad, ready to come with me. Any moment. Smartly, now."

"Yes, sir."

The superintendent picked up the telephone on his desk. "Operator—get me a line to the Chief Operating Superintendent, British Railways, Waverley Station, Edinburgh. Quickly. You have that? Priority. Right."

Ian found the police officer looking at him sternly, over the telephone.

"So I take it, in your mature view, that you don't consider poaching salmon to be a very serious offence, young man?"

"Oh . . . er . . . well." Unprepared for this, Ian blinked and stammered. "I suppose it is, really. But . . ."

"You aided and abetted a poacher to avoid the police, it seems to me. In fact, by supplying him with food and assistance, you made yourselves accessories to his offence, eh?"

Ian swallowed. "We . . . we helped an injured man in trouble, sir. We could hardly do anything else. And, anyway—he wasn't really poaching, you see. So we can't have been accessories to a crime that wasn't committed. Can we?"

The superintendent's steely eyes twinkled. "That's quite a thought, isn't it!"

The sergeant reappeared at the door. "Sir—the man bought a second-class single to Liverpool. The train is due at Newcastleton at 2.19 and at Carlisle at 2.57."

"And what about Riccarton Junction?"

"That's an unscheduled halt, sir, for water. It should be there by about 2.5."

"It's 1.57 now." The superintendent drummed his fingers on his desk. "Look, Sergeant—I can't wait for the Chief Operating Super in Edinburgh. I'm dealing with this myself. When he comes through on the phone, tell him that we want that train slowed down. Not actually halted, you understand? If it stops for a long period, our man may take fright and bolt. I want the train to be slowed, stopped for short spells at a time, as though there was some obstruction on the line. So that he doesn't get suspicious. It isn't a busy line, fortunately. To give us time to catch up with him. I reckon we should be up with it before it gets out of the hills—before it actually crosses the Border. Then phone Cumberland County Police, and tell them what I'm doing. To have people ready to search the train at Carlisle, in case anything goes wrong. Right?"

"Yessir. You'll know where the train is? I mean, where it's halted for you?"

"We'll see it. The road and the railway run side by side all the way down Liddesdale. I'll keep in touch with you by radio-telephone. Better get Inspector Scott in, if you can." The superintendent reached for his silver-braided peaked cap. "Right, young fellow—come along!"

Ian had been terrified that he would, in fact, have been left behind there at the police station. He was out of that door and down the stairs like a scalded cat. The superintendent followed with rather more dignity.

Two big, black, powerful cars, Jaguars, stood outside the main office, beside Ian's bicycle, engines already running. Four policemen sat upright in the rear one, with its POLICE notice in blue lights and its wireless aerial; in that to the front sat the uniformed driver, Macphail.

"Into the back with you," the superintendent said, pointing to the first car. He himself got in beside the driver. Before the doors had slammed shut, Macphail had let in his clutch and they were off.

"Step on it," the driver was told briefly. "Up Slitrig, by Shankend, and over the summit for Newcastleton. Hard as you like."

"Aye, sir."

Through the narrow streets of Rulekirk they threaded, the great cars as it were straining at the leash. But once out on to the open road, their impatient purring swiftly changed to a deep-throated roar as the two vehicles leapt free. Snorting and snarling like huge cats, they swept up the long, twisting valley of the Slitrig Water, southwards.

Ian could not possibly remain sitting down in the back. Standing, eyes glistening, his face peering between the two sets of broad, blue-coated shoulders in front, his glance swivelled between the speedometer and the uncoiling ribbon of road that seemed to unroll before them.

CHAPTER ELEVEN

Solo Performance

Don stood panting in the corridor of the third-last coach of the south-bound train, after he had slammed the door shut behind him. He saw the end of Rulekirk Station platform tail away, and the parapet of the high bridge across the Teviot take its place, and suddenly he felt horribly alone, not at all sure of himself—and, to tell the truth, thoroughly scared. He had acted wholely on impulse, on the spur of the moment, without any attempt to count the cost. Now, here he was with the bill to pay, alone on a train bound for England, without a ticket, without money to pay for one, attempting to dog a rough-looking and unpleasant character whom he believed to be a dangerous criminal. Abruptly he felt weak at the knees. Why on earth had he done it? What on earth had he let himself in for? What business of his was it if the Countess of Whatever-it-was had her jewels stolen? If Mickey Pat's companion in crime had run out on him? If it looked as though justice was not going to be done? All that was the police's affair, wasn't it? It was no real responsibility of one Don MacDonald at all, was it? And yet, here he was, heading inevitably for trouble, real trouble, whatever happened. What an idiot he had been!

It was being alone that was the worst of it, of course. If he had still had Ian with him, he probably would not have felt this way, at all.

Since his knees did not feel as though they would continue to support him, he had to sit down. The compartment nearest to the door was empty, and he went in and sank down on the seat, to stare out somewhat blindly as the last suburbs of Rulekirk died away amongst the steeply-sloping green hillsides that hemmed in the town on all sides.

It was the sight of an ordinary, scarlet telephone kiosk that eventually made him take a grip on himself. Something about it standing there at a road-end as they rumbled past, looking so normal, so much a part of the usual, ordered scheme of things, helped him to see his own position more sensibly. After all, he wasn't in any real trouble. Not yet. Not serious trouble. Nothing that the telephone, for instance, would not solve. Ian would tell the police what was happening; they would telephone the next station—or maybe the next again—and the train might be held up. Or if that was too much to hope for, they might put a couple of policemen aboard, somewhere, and then everything would be out of his hands. Even if they weren't absolutely convinced about Dubitsky and didn't feel like actually arresting him, he himself could get out of it easily enough. At some station. Not too far on. His aunt, telephoned, would vouch for him, and would pay the railway fare. It wouldn't be so very much. He might get a bit of a ticking-off, but that would be all. A ticking-off wasn't going to hurt him . . .

Feeling better every moment, Don rapidly became more like his normal self in that he began to plan further action rather than content himself with sitting still. Since he *had* gone so far, he had better do something to justify it all, he decided. Whatever happened, there was no point in sitting there and staring out of the window.

Getting up, he moved out into the corridor.

The corridor was empty—as was the next compartment. It seemed to be a pretty empty train altogether. Not that that was very unusual. He tried hard to see again, in his mind's eye, the point in the long train where Dubitsky had climbed aboard. He should have taken exact note of it, of course—but he had been far too excited. He thought that probably it was not this coach he was in, but the next one, towards the front. But this end of it. He could not be sure, but that was the way that he seemed to remember it.

Slowly, cautiously, yet trying to look quite casual, he began to move along the corridor. He discovered that, by examining the somewhat dirty glass of the windows he could see, by reflection, whether there was anybody sitting in each compartment before he actually reached it. That was a help. With luck, it meant that he need not really show himself.

He found two ladies sitting together in one non-smoking compartment, and a soldier alone and asleep in the next. That was all in his own coach. Almost tiptoeing now, in his caution, Don edged his way through the little alleyway that linked the coaches.

The first compartment beyond was empty. There was somebody in the next, however. Don crouched down, almost leaning his head against the outer window in order to obtain the fullest slantwise reflection from the compartment beyond. Yes—it was his man. The dark, hatchet-like features and the long sideburns were unmistakable. He was sitting, back to the engine, alone, in the far corner, looking out of that window in the other direction.

Don slipped into the first compartment, and sat down again.

What now? He could only wait and watch. And hope. Hope, amongst other things, that Dubitsky would remain where he was and not decide to come strolling along the corridor this way—for then he could hardly fail to notice Don and recognise him, surely, even though he was to stand and stare out of the other window, back turned.

Don found that if he sat near the middle of the seat, facing the engine, he could, by just leaning over a little, see Dubitsky in his corner reflected in the corridor window. Did that mean that Dubitsky could likewise see him, if he looked? Don was not quite sure about that—though it seemed probable. He moved just a little farther over, just in case, so that he would not be visible, but by leaning slightly to the left he could keep an eye on the reflection of his quarry.

Suddenly Don realised that they had just passed through a station without stopping. Stobs, it was called. One chance gone of getting off the train. Not that he felt like doing so now. Having got his man under observation, like this.

He was thankful that the train was not going very fast. Every minute counted, to give Ian time to tell the police and get things moving. Obviously they were climbing a long ascent, with the hills closing in all round. They were deep in the Cheviots, and Don knew enough about the general geography to realise that they would climb for quite a long way and to quite a high altitude before they got over the summit and began the long slant down Liddesdale to the lower country around the Solway estuary. The longer, and slower, the better.

He kept leaning sideways to take a quick look at the reflection from the next compartment. Dubitsky appeared to stare pretty steadily out of the far window. Only once or twice he glanced at a piece of paper—no doubt Mickey Pat's spurned letter.

Don had to make up his mind, if he could, as to possible courses of action. If he saw Dubitsky stirring, getting to his feet, he would himself get up, in case the man came along the corridor this way, and stand with his back turned, looking out of the window. In fact, if he had the window open, he could actually be leaning out—which perhaps would make him less recognisable as one of the boys on Rulekirk platform. He stood up, and quietly let down the door window to half-open.

What would he do if Dubitsky got out at some wayside station? Hurry along the corridor and get out as far away from the man as he could? It wouldn't be so bad if other people were getting out too. But it was going to be tricky if they were alone, or almost. It was very empty wild country. Suppose he was to climb down on the *other* side, the far side of the train? Then up on to the opposite platform—hidden by the train itself. He could perhaps dodge the ticket collector that way, too. But that would only work at a very small station, probably, where the two or three members of the staff concentrated on the side where the train had come in. Otherwise he would just get into worse trouble than ever. He could only wait and see.

When the train chugged through another small station—Shankend it was named—without stopping, Don began to feel just a little bit worried. If this was an express, not going to stop at any intermediate stations, then it was not going to give Ian and the police much time to do anything. Once over the summit, it would soon change from this heavy pulling and make up for lost time, thundering down the equally long slope to Carlisle, non-stop. Don had to admit that the thought of himself being carried away all that distance, and over into England, was not pleasant. Somehow, as long as he remained in his own Scotland, it did not seem quite so bad . . .

Presently the train's ascent became noticeably easier, the engine's puffing efforts less laboured. Presumably they had reached the summit of the pass—though the steep hills all around looked no different. They did not seem to be actually gathering speed, however, as he had expected. In fact . . . yes, those were the brakes being applied. They were slowing down.

The reflection of movement in the corridor glass caught his eye. Dubitsky was rising to his feet. Don watched tensely. Was this a station, and was the man getting ready to do a bunk? Or was he just wondering why they were slowing down?

Dubitsky stood at his window—and so did Don. It was a station that they were approaching, sure enough—though what place it might serve in this hilly desolation was not evident. It was a bare, bleak spot, with only one or two houses, that looked as though they were connected with the railway itself. Don hoped that he didn't have to get off there and do any trailing of the fugitive—for there didn't appear to be enough cover to hide a sparrow.

As more and more of the platform went past, Don wondered if they were not going to stop after all.

Riccarton Junction, he saw the place was called. Far back on the train as they were, they were almost at the southern end of the platform before they finally clanked to a halt.

Don waited, hand on the door handle, ready.

Nothing happened. No sound came from next door of window or door being opened. Neither Dubitsky nor anybody else seemed to be getting out here. Don let his breath go in a sigh of relief.

He opened his own window a little farther, quietly, and put his head out. Up in front was a large water-tower with the usual dripping sleeve stretching over to the panting engine. So that was it! He might have guessed. Merely a halt to water the engine after the long ascent. No doubt the boiler needed it, too.

All too soon the watering was done, however, and they moved forward again.

Presumably they were now going downhill—or at least, along the level? Yet the train did not seem to pick up speed, nevertheless; indeed it was only chuntering along now. Not that Don complained about that. But he wondered . . . ?

After rumbling on very leisurely for perhaps another five minutes, the train ground to a halt again—this time nowhere in particular amongst the empty hills. In a few seconds Don heard Dubitsky's window go down with a slam, as no doubt he thrust his head out to see what was delaying them.

They moved on again—but still slowly, haltingly.

Don was almost sure, now, that this was not accidental. Had the engine-driver received some message back at Riccarton Junction telling him to slow down? It looked like it. This was not a busy route, over empty heather moorland, and there seemed to be no good reason why they should be crawling like this. Don's spirits now were steadily rising.

Apparently the same could not be said for the passenger next door. Don could hear Dubitsky pacing his compartment—whether suspecting trouble or merely impatient was not to be known. The boy was beginning to worry that the other might come out into the corridor for greater freedom of pacing, and so discover him, when with a great jangling and clanking the train drew up once more—again on an open stretch of line.

Either there was something far wrong with the railway system—or this was Ian's work. This time, as Don stared out of the window, biting his lip in excitement, movement up on the long, bare, heathery hillside caught his eye. Two black shapes, moving fast. It must be a road up there—the main road. Over a mile away, probably. Yes, back on the skyline he could see silhouetted a line of telegraph poles. The road itself was not apparent from down here in the valley.

Those two swiftly-moving shapes were black cars, long and low-set. Don's heart bounded. Could they be police cars? They were the right shape and colour. And they looked urgent, somehow—determined. And going very fast, obviously. Or was he imagining things? Wishful thinking? Or even just coincidence?

Don heard sudden movement in the next compartment. Stepping back, to make use of his precious reflection, he saw that Dubitsky was up again and staring likewise out of the far window towards those speeding black shapes on the hill. Something about the man's tense attitude there was very telling. He also had decided that they were police cars.

Now, what?

Back at the window Don watched the cars' progress. There was a lot of hillside between them and the railway—boggy rising heather ground. No sign of any side-road to bring them in this direction. Police might be on the job, less than a mile away—but it would be quite some time before they could actually join the train. Time for Dubitsky to do . . . what?

Don moved back to mid-compartment again, turning to peer for the reflection. As he did so, his breath caught in his throat. The reflection was clear enough—all too clear. Dubitsky was standing exactly as he was himself, gazing this way, almost crouching indeed. Without the least doubt he was seeing Don as he himself saw the man.

After that, events happened swiftly. In a few strides Dubitsky was out of his compartment and into Don's, fists clenched, sallow features grim.

"You!" he jerked, grabbing the boy's arm. "You one of those boys! You follow me. You . . . you

"You!" he jerked, grabbing the boy's arm.

stinking spy!" he added something vigorous and unpleasant in a foreign tongue, and wrenched Don's shoulder, shaking him.

"I . . . I . . ." Don swallowed. "Take your hands off me!" he exclaimed a little shrilly. "You're hurting me."

"I hurt you more . . . !"

"You'd better not! The police . . . the police are on to you now! Out there. You saw them? Those cars . . ." Don knew that he was gabbling. He was much afraid—for Dubitsky was looking alarmingly savage, and was twisting his arm painfully.

"So! The police . . . you tell! *You!*" Without warning, Dubitsky lashed out a vicious back-handed swipe that caught Don across the side of the face and flung him backwards staggering, so that he fell over the seat. The man came after him.

Don had been frightened before—but now he was angry. He was still afraid, of course—but that blow had made him furious as well. From his half-lying position he lashed out at his assailant with knees and fists.

"You no' . . . tell police . . . more!" the other grunted, hitting and being hit. He got in a blow to Don's jaw that set flashes jumping before his eyes and made his head reel.

The boy opened his mouth. "Help!" he yelled. "Help!"

A hand closed over his lips—and Don bit hard. Then,

as the other fist drove in at him again, he wrenched away, and wriggling, slid sideways down to the floor, where he coiled himself, in a sort of rugby tackle, round the man's legs. Dubitsky had to turn round, in order to stoop to free himself—and abruptly paused, straightening up. A woman was staring at them in astonishment from the corridor.

For a moment or two it was as though all of them were frozen, like a cinema film that had stuck and become merely a still, man, woman and boy, motionless.

Don recovered himself first. "Help!" he called out to the woman. "Get help! Quick! This man . . . !"

The startled lady gulped, raised an unsteady hand to her mouth, and then set off up the train at almost a run.

Dubitsky also came to life. He kicked out violently, to free his legs from Don's clutch, slightly winding the boy in the process. Then, leaping over his fallen victim's body, he stumbled out into the corridor, and was gone.

Don slowly picked himself up, breathless, feeling sick and dazed, and sat down heavily on the seat. He was vaguely aware of the outer window of the next compartment being run down again, and the door being flung open with a slam. Gasping for breath, he tried to collect his scattered wits.

He sat there only for a few moments. Then, lightheaded, he got to his feet, and lurched to his own window, to peer out and down.

Dubitsky was down there, on hands and knees, on the cinder path of the railway track. He had jumped down. It seemed a long way down, without a platform. His bag lay on the grass beyond him, obviously thrown out. The man seemed to be scrabbling there. Then, even as Don watched, he got to his feet, grabbed his bag, and, limping slightly, set off back along the line at a run.

The moment of decision had arrived for Don MacDonald. Action, undoubtedly, was required of him now, slightly sick and befuddled as he felt. Blinking hard, and taking a long deep breath, he pulled his window right down, and put his hand out to turn the door handle.

CHAPTER TWELVE

The Hunt is On

Action at last! Ian could scarcely keep himself from shouting aloud. For what seemed ages he had hardly dared to think of Don, of what his brother must be doing and thinking and feeling as the train rumbled through the hills, carrying him farther and farther away from the country that they knew, drawing ever nearer to the English border, to real trouble. All the time Ian had felt that he was failing him terribly, that he was caught in a net of utter stupidity and disbelief, that nothing would ever come right. But now, action at last.

And what action it was! Never had Ian known motoring like this. He had travelled fast before, in his father's car. He had even ridden thrillingly and for a long way in a police Jaguar, up in the Highlands when they were taken home after the battle with the deer poachers. But on neither occasion had they been racing against anything, against time and a train.

The only slight disappointment about that whirlwind journey through the Border hills was that the big cars did not in fact seem to be going quite so fast as they actually did—good driving, extra power, and superb road-holding qualities being responsible for that. At times, with the speedometer touching ninety-five, Ian could hardly believe it. Fortunately there was very little traffic on that lonely highway through the empty, fifty-mile belt of hills—and what there was, well warned by the frequent blaring of horns, wisely gave them all the room possible.

They climbed and climbed, up out of the river valleys, up through the long heather slopes and on to the bald, windswept ridges where even the sheep were left behind and only the wailing curlews and long-eared mountain hares lived. On the way, the superintendent spoke several times into the radio-telephone fixed on the dashboard in front of him. He spoke to the car behind, and to other patrol cars scattered over the Border area; he was in contact with the station sergeant back at Rulekirk, who informed him that the railway people up in Edinburgh were co-operating gladly, and that from Riccarton Junction onwards the train would be only limping towards Carlisle; and once, when Ian suddenly remembered Don's bicycle, still lying outside Rulekirk railway station, he amusedly gave orders for a van to pick it up, collect Ian's own, and have them ready to take to their aunt's house at Denholm.

"It's a wonderful thing, that R.T.," Ian said admiringly.

"It has its uses, yes," the officer agreed with Ian.

Gravel spurting from under screaming tyres, they roared over the summit of the watershed at 1200 feet above sea level, at Limekiln Edge, the very tail-end of the spine of Scotland, with all the streams behind them flowing down to the Teviot, the Tweed, and the North Sea, and those in front running into the Solway and the Atlantic. The superintendent pointed away over to their left, down some way across the short heather and moss, where the narrow black line of the railway disappeared into a tunnel through the hill.

"A long stiff pull up for a train," he said. "Nine hundred feet rise in twelve miles. Just as well for us, eh?"

Although they were actually going downhill now, safe driving in fact forced them to reduce speed somewhat. Even so, they did not dawdle. Now their road crossed the railway and drew away from it to the west. In a minute or two the superintendent was pointing again and consulting his watch.

"Riccarton Junction over there. You can just see it, where those two hills join. Not what you usually think of as a railway junction, eh? Where the lines fork for Liddesdale and Tynedale, that's all. A platform, a few houses, and the water tanks. It's them that are important for us. Locomotives need a long drink after climbing all this way. There may have been as much as ten minutes delay there. It's 2.16 now.

That means we've covered that last fifteen miles in sixteen minutes. Not too bad considering the road. The train probably only left here five or six minutes ago."

"Goodness—as little as that?" Suddenly Don seemed to be comfortingly near at hand.

"Yes. And the driver will have had his instructions to go slow, at Riccarton. So, perhaps in another five or six miles . . ."

In fact, it was considerably less when, suddenly, they saw the train. It was a faint column of dark smoke that they glimpsed first, rising out of a valley. Then rounding a corner they could see the whole train. It was stopped, on a straight stretch of line amongst the brown hills—but well over a mile away from them, across the rough heather.

"What's the idiot stopped there for?" the superintendent demanded. "We can't get near his train there, in the cars. We'll have to go scrambling over all that heather—in full view of the fugitive. This is ridiculous."

"Maybe the driver's just having one of these wee stops. Like you said. To delay things," Ian suggested. "He maybe doesn't think that we're as far on as we are."

"Perhaps you're right, boy."

It seemed that Ian was, for almost at once a few puffs of white steam came from the engine, and then the train started slowly on its way once more.

The police cars rapidly overhauled it now. But the road was separated from the railway by at least half a mile of heather, and drawing no nearer.

"There's a side road, sir, branches off in about a mile. To the left. Passes over a railway bridge, and joins the main Liddesdale road," Macphail mentioned. "If the driver's seen us now, likely that's where he's making for."

"Let's hope so. The trouble is, if he's seen us, probably this Dubitsky has seen us too."

They swung off on to the side road a minute later. Sure enough, as they dipped down, they could see for a moment the train halted, where the road crossed the railway half a mile away.

That half mile, however, took longer to cover than two or three of the previous miles. The road was narrow and winding and unfenced. Sheep seemed to love it, the lambs always preferring the opposite side from their mothers until just before the cars were upon them. Some actually slept contentedly in the middle. Half-way to the railway line there was a ford to cross, over a fast-running burn. The two Jaguars crept along, snorting impatiently.

At last they reached the bridge and the waiting train beneath. Waving to the engine driver who was leaning out of his cab, the superintendent jumped out of his car, climbed the low wall, and hurried down the embankment into the cutting, Ian at his heels. Three policemen were not far behind.

A man came running down towards them from the rear of the train. It was the guard.

"Och, you're too late, sir," he called out. "Your man's awa'. He got off back there, where we were stopped before."

"Confound it!" the superintendent cried. "What d'you mean, man—got off?"

"He must have seen your cars, sir. Same as we did. Up the hill. Him and the laddie. He jumped down on to the metals, and went running back the line. The laddie after him. Och, I shouted at them to stop, but it was no use . . ."

"You say the boy was with him?"

"Aye. At least, he was behind him, sir. Running after him."

"Good old Don!" Ian exclaimed. "He's still keeping tabs on him!"

"And they went back along the line, you say? Did you see how far?"

"Och, they stuck to the line till they were round a bit bend. Couldna see any more then. We brought the train along here, sir, as the nearest place we could speak to you."

"Yes. Of course. Very sensible." But the superintendent was frowning. "This is a pest, if you like! We can't get the cars anywhere along there. We're well over a mile from where you stopped before, here. Guard—could you back the train along? Take us there. Quickly? The line will be clear behind you, won't it?"

The other looked hesitant. "Well, sir—it's against regulations. The line'll be clear, right enough. Control know this train's being held up. I suppose we might . . ."

"I'll take responsibility, man. Tell your engine driver. Quick." The superintendent raised his voice. "Macphail!" he shouted. "Phone Sergeant Hogarth. Tell him to inform Chief Operating Super, Edinburgh, that we're backing this train for over a mile. Essential. Our man's bolted back at the last stop. Then warn all patrol cars to close in on this area. Better get Hogarth to send a squad out in a couple of vans. We may have to comb these confounded hills. Got that?"

They saw Macphail's hand wave from the first car.

"Right—along to the guard's van, all of you," the superintendent ordered. Ian scuttled ahead, determined on no account to be left out of this. The guard himself came trotting along behind. All along the train anxious passengers peered down from open windows.

They climbed up the high step into the guard's van. The guard stood outside on the step, leaning over and out, so that the driver could see his signals. Clanking and jerking, the train started to move backwards.

"This brother of yours seems to be quite a boy," the superintendent mentioned. "Might even make a sort of half-decent policeman one day."

"Oh, no," Ian told him seriously. "He's going to be a civil engineer."

"D'you tell me that, now! Well, well—another good man gone wrong, eh? Maybe he's got the rights of it, though. What about yourself, young man?"

"Well, I'm very keen on history, and that sort of thing, you know. Research."

"Just the job for our Criminal Records Department! All long-haired antiquaries in there!" He turned to the guard. "Anything special about the stretch of line round this bend? I mean, where these two disappeared?"

"No, sir. Just the usual open hillside."

"Nowhere that this man could hide up?"

"Don't think so. What's he done, this man, sir?"

"Suspected jewel robbery and car theft."

"D'you tell me that? And the laddie?"

"This boy's brother." The police officer smiled slightly. "Tailing him. On, h'm, behalf of the police."

"Jings!"

"I do hope . . . I do hope that Don's all right," Ian said. "I mean, that this Stefan hasn't turned on him. When he saw he was being followed. Attacked him, or anything . . . "

"I shouldn't think so. He'll have been far too busy trying to put distance between himself and us."

"But if he saw that Don would be able to bring us down on to him . . . ?"

"No use worrying, son. We'll be there soon, anyway."

"This train's going terribly slowly, isn't it?"

"I wouldn't say that—considering it's going backwards. So you're interested in history, are you. Scots history?"

"Of course." Ian realised that the superintendent was trying to take his mind off Don's position. He tried to talk history as they trundled back along that line—but it was not a great success.

At last they turned the bend, which the guard said was the one round which he had seen Dubitsky and Don disappear. A long straight stretch of line reached northwards across the hillside. It was completely empty, with no sign of life or movement on the flanking hillsides.

"M'mm. No sign of anyone," the superintendent said, frowning. "We ought to be seeing something of them, surely? How long have they had—since they bolted? It can't be more than ten or twelve minutes, at the outside. We can see a couple of miles from here, at least. You wouldn't think that they would have run that far . . ."

"I hope—oh, I hope Don's all right!" Ian exclaimed, biting his lip.

A pity I didn't bring a pair of field-glasses," the superintendent muttered.

"Dubitsky wouldn't just keep running back along the line anyway, would he?"

"It's easier going than amongst the heather and those steep braesides. He probably could cover much more ground than on the hill. I expect his idea's to put as much distance as he can between himself and where he left the train."

"But with Don behind him? He would be bound to *know* Don was there, wouldn't he? He would be sure to look back? You . . . you don't think that he might have turned on him, on Don? To, to attack him?"

"No, no. Anyway, your brother wouldn't just wait for him, if he tried anything of the sort. I've no doubt he can run just as fast as this Dubitsky. And that would only have delayed them . . . "

The guard, still leaning out on the step of his van, interrupted. "Hey—there's somebody up there! Look!"

Away, high above them, on a slight ridge of the heathery hill, a tiny figure danced about and waved its arms crazily—like something from a Punch and Judy show.

"It's Don!" Ian cried. "It's Don!"

"Stop the train, Guard!" the superintendent exclaimed. " He's trying to attract our attention. This is where we leave you. Once we're down, you can get on your way. Thanks for your co-operation. Sorry you've been delayed." He turned to the three constables. " Well, you fellows—this is where you start getting your weight down! We're going climbing!"

CHAPTER THIRTEEN

Fugitive in the Heather

Quite suddenly authority, experience and superb equipment, the inventions of modern science and all the rest of it, so important and impressive since leaving Rulekirk, took a back seat. None of these was of any great value in getting up that long hillside. It was not very steep, but the old heather was fairly high, and near the foot, at least, the ground was wet and soggy. Everything was reversed from the order of the chase so far. Ian led the way, well up in front, actually running, lightly, easily: then came the three constables, straggling out, going with heavy determination; and a bad fifth came the superintendent, the oldest man present, growing red-faced and breathless.

Ian, used to climbing much higher Highland hills than these, was up to his brother before the superintendent was much more than half way.

"Don!" he cried. "Are you all right? Oh, I'm glad to see you! Where is he?"

"You've been absolutely ages!" Don shouted back. "I thought you were never coming. Yes, I'm all right. At least . . . now, I am. He's just over there—over this ridge."

"Oh, good." Ian came up, panting only slightly. "Sorry we were so long, Don. I had an awful job convincing the police. At first. Once I got taken to the superintendent it was all right. That's him at the foot there. He's decent. But we fairly moved once we got started. We touched ninety-seven miles an hour, once! In a Jaguar. It was marvellous! But . . . what's happened with Dubitsky? Did he try to hurt you? Attack you, or anything? You look a bit bashed."

"Well . . . he did hit me once or twice. I'm all right. It's mainly dust off the carriage floor, I think. That was before he jumped off, and ran along the line. I kept . . . well, sort of well behind him, after that! I didn't get too close . . ."

"Golly—I should say not! It was in the train that he hit you?"

"Yes. I was in the next compartment. It was empty. Half the train was empty. But don't bother about that, now. Look—don't go any farther up, Ian. We're just below the ridge here, and he can't see us."

"But he'll be getting farther and farther away."

"No. He's hiding. In some peat-hags. At least, he's been there for ten minutes or so. When I came up to the ridge first, his back was turned to me, and when I saw where he was heading, I dropped flat. So I don't think he knows that I've seen him go to ground."

"And you think he's still there?"

"Yes. He was a minute ago, anyway. He's not very fit, actually—not really able for this sort of thing. And he's carrying his bag, of course. Not fit like those deer poachers. Recovering from his accident, I suppose."

The first of the constables came puffing up. Him, also, Don warned to keep this side of the little ridge. He, indeed, and his two companions when they reached him, were glad enough of any excuse for a breather. They were sweating and scarlet in their thick uniforms. There was no unnecessary conversation just then.

As Ian explained the position, Don crept back to the crest of the ridge, and flat on his stomach, peered over. He came back in a moment or two.

"Still there," he reported. "At least, you can't see him—but you *could* if he'd moved away. It's open all round."

They had to wait some time for the superintendent. He looked quite exhausted. He did not say a word while Ian introduced his brother, and together they poured out the story. At length, nodding, he took off his flat, diced cap, and telling his men to do the same, moved forward to the crest. On hands and knees they all looked cautiously over.

The land dropped away slightly before them into a shallow valley, and then rose beyond, up and up to a high hill, bare and open. All the area in sight, indeed, was bare and open—except for the actual floor of the little valley. There the heather and peat was cut up by the action of water and ice and wind into deep moss-hags, lots of little cliffs and clefts and hollows in the peat, black and wet and unpleasant.

Don pointed. "In there," he said. "If he'd moved out, we could see him. It's all so open. No cover anywhere else."

"Yes. But . . . where?" the superintendent panted. "A mighty . . . lot of . . . that peat stuff. And he could have . . . worked down . . . the valley. Still amongst it."

"I don't think so," Don said. "And if he did, we could follow his tracks in the peat mud. I know just where he went in. You see that very green patch, up on the hillside opposite? Shaped like a triangle. Well, five o'clock from that, down into the peat-hags. You'll see a big hag, with a sort of top-knot of heather growing out of it. Well—just to the left of that. In that huddle of small stuff. He's in there."

"M'mmm. Well, young fellow—you seem to have it all taped! Now—how to winkle him out of there? The moment we show ourselves, here, he'll be off up the hill beyond. And I must admit, however spry you two may be, I'm not just in training for this sort of thing!" He glanced at his three constables. "I don't know that my men are likely to be any faster on their feet than this character is. We may lose him again."

"Yes," Don admitted. "But, see—if Ian and I were to go round. Work up to the right, here, on this side of the ridge, and over behind that shoulder of hill there, out of sight—we could come down on him from above. Over there. Letting him see us, and you staying hidden here. Then, if he bolted, it would be either back here, or down the valley . . ."

"And if you sent two policemen down to the left, so as to move down into the valley to cut him off if he went that way, then you'd have him," Ian put in. "Between us, we'd drive him into your arms, if you stay hidden."

"All worked out, eh? You boys seem to know a bit about hillcraft?"

"We go a lot to the Highlands—where deer-stalking goes on," Ian explained. "It's the same principle, really."

"Indeed! I suppose it is. Well, it's as good a plan as any." Undoubtedly the superintendent was likely to be in favour of any plan which allowed him to remain where he was meantime. "But, remember—we can't be sure that our man will stay conveniently where he is while you two are working your way round."

"Oh, no. Of course not."

"Listen—keep your ears open for our police whistles, then. You'll hear them—they carry a long way. Here's the code. If we blow short single blasts, then he's moving, and heading straight up the hill. Towards you. A succession of longer blasts means he's moving right—though that's not likely I think. And long sustained whistling means left, down the valley. Got that?"

"Yes. Short, uphill. Longer blasts, up the valley. Steady whistling, down the way. That it?"

"Fine. Off you go, then. And rather you than me! Good luck!"

Backing away, the boys went hurrying to the right, where their ridge rose steadily until it turned into a knobbly shoulder of the hill. Behind this, always keeping the bulk of it between them and the peat-hag valley, they skirted, until they reckoned that they were to the east of where Dubitsky was hiding, whereas before they had been to the west. It was not a very big circuit, really, for the hill itself was not very big. Breathing deeply, nevertheless, they moved up to the new crest, and looked over.

From up here they could see the policemen away below them. Two had gone down the ridge for about two hundred yards, ready to run over and down into the valley if necessary. The other two lay where they had been. There was no sign of movement amongst the moss-hags.

"Well—we just get up and walk down openly, I suppose," Don said. "It will seem sort of funny . . ."

It did feel distinctly strange, after all the hiding and secrecy, to be strolling unconcealedly down that hillside towards the man's hiding-place. They felt very brazen, somehow. And uncomfortable. Was this such a good idea, after all, they began to wonder? Perhaps Dubitsky would come *towards* them, away from the policemen? Perhaps he wouldn't bolt at all, but lie still, hoping not to be discovered? Perhaps he was not even there, now . . .

They walked on, and nothing happened.

They were two-thirds of the way down to the floor of the valley, and feeling complete fools, before suddenly a figure rose up amongst the peat-hags. He shouted something at them, and shook his fist angrily. Then he turned and went, plunging and slithering on the slippery peat-mud, down the valley, threading his way amongst the hags, bag in hand.

"I was sure he was still there!" Don gasped.

"He's chosen to go that way. I suppose he doesn't want to get back into sight of the railway . . ."

The two constables farther down let Dubitsky get perhaps seventy yards nearer to them. Then they rose up, and went running heavily down to intercept him.

The hunted man paused there amongst the mosses for a moment, at sight of them. Then he turned left, more than left, and went plunging across the peat, eastwards, straight towards the hidden superintendent.

The boys stood still, holding their breath.

Dubitsky was only a bare ten yards away when the superintendent jumped to his feet, a little to one side, the constable a little to the other. The fugitive stopped in his tracks, flung a desperate glance behind him, around him. Then, suddenly seeming to grow smaller, to shrink in on himself, he dropped his bag to the ground, and stood where he was, waiting, hands at his sides, head sinking, a seemingly beaten man.

The chase was over.

It took a little while for the brothers to reach the rest of the party, for they had to cross the peat. When they did come up, rather muddy now, Dubitsky was already handcuffed between two constables. He had quite enough spirit left to scowl blackly at the two boys, however.

The superintendent was not looking as triumphant as might be expected, himself. "Well, you two—we've got your man," he greeted them, frowning. "All very nice and according to plan. Except that there are no jewels!"

"No . . . no jewels?"

"You mean—nothing?"

The boys stood staring.

"Not a thing. We've gone over him—all of him. He's carrying nothing even suspicious. We found your letter from the Irishman. That's all."

"You looked in his bag?"

"Naturally. This is distinctly awkward, you will realise? It makes the position somewhat difficult."

Dubitsky obviously realised that very well. Glancing quickly from the brothers to the police officer, he spoke up, thickly. "What right you do this to me? Chase me here. I nothing do wrong. This boys, they make trouble. What for you come after me?"

"I told you," the superintendent said gruffly. "Suspected jewel robbery and car theft."

"I have no jewels. I have no car. If I have car I not go in train. You no right chasing me."

"Why did you jump off the train and run away, man?"

The prisoner hesitated only for a moment. "I remember something I leave. At the camp. Brackenhope. Something important. I want to go back for it."

"A likely story!"

"I try leave train at that place. Where they get water for train. Riccarton. But they no let me go there. Say not a station. So when train stops later I go off . . ."

"That's not right," Don objected. "I was in the next compartment all the time. Watching. And listening. He didn't try to get off at Riccarton Junction. Nobody stopped him, for he didn't speak to anybody the whole time. Except me."

"This boy is a bad boy. A liar," Dubitsky declared. "Or a fool. He mistakes me for other man, maybe. I never see him before to-day. He runs after me. I complain of this boy. He makes much trouble for me . . ."

"All right, all right," the superintendent cut him short. "Complaints can wait. Any complaints you can make at the police station."

"But . . . you cannot take me to the police station. It is not right. I do nothing wrong."

"It's an offence to leave or enter a railway train except at the duly authorised stops and platforms," the officer said grimly. "That'll do in the meantime. Take him along, men."

"And he attacked me, too. That's an offence, isn't it?" Don pointed out.

"But what about the jewels?" Ian cried. "We've got to find the jewels."

"The point has not escaped me," the superintendent said sarcastically as Dubitsky was led away downhill. "But that will have to wait, too—assuming that this man had them in the first instance. There's no proof of that, mind. Only your hunch. You may be right—but you may not. The car theft may have had nothing whatever to do with the jewel robbery."

"Oh, but it has—obviously!" Don protested. "Everything links up."

"Except the jewels, boy—except the jewels! And meantime, all the county's police are searching for this man. Cumberland, too. The railway people are up in the air. I've got to call things off and tidy things up. I'll have to get down to the radio in my car."

"Yes, but the jewels—they must be *somewhere!*" Ian insisted. "Dubitsky was running away. I don't mean only from the train, just now. But before. When he got *on* the train. He was bolting. He wasn't having anything more to do with Mickey Pat. He wouldn't do that just because of the wrecked car. He wanted the jewels for himself—all of them. Perhaps . . . perhaps he might have left them in the train?"

"No. Why should he?" Don objected. "He would never do that. He brought his bag away. The jewels would be in his pocket, I expect. Why leave them behind? He'd never see them again."

"They needn't have been on him, at all," the superintendent pointed out. "If he had them in the first place. He could have hidden them somewhere. At Brackenhope. Anywhere. Passed them on to some receiver. Even sent them ahead of him, through the post."

"Would you have risked that, sir—with stuff worth thousands and thousands of pounds?"

"Probably not. But then I wouldn't have stolen the jewels, or the car. I wouldn't have deserted my mate. I wouldn't have bolted from the train like that. I just haven't Dubitsky's mental make-up."

"Could he have hidden them, somehow, after leaving the train?" Ian asked.

"No. Not without me seeing him," his brother answered. "I never let him out of my sight. Until up here. At the peat-hags." He stopped. "That's it—the peat-hags! He's left them there, buried there somewhere, for a bet! When he saw us coming down the hill. He'd realise then that the game was nearly up . . ."

"Of course. Seeing the two of us," Ian broke in.

"Before, there had only been you. For me to be with you, up there, must have told him that he was surrounded. I couldn't have got there alone. So he would hide the jewels there in the peat-mud, and make a bolt for it. And if he was caught, he would have drawn the scent away, at least. And not have anything found on him."

The superintendent was already walking across the tussocky grass towards the edge of the peat-hags.

At the black rim of it, he paused distastefully. "Dirty, mucky stuff!" he objected.

"Oh, it's not so bad," Ian assured. "If you sort of skim over it, with a skating kind of movement, you don't really sink in."

"And it washes off, of course," Don added.

"Thanks," their companion said. "I'll take your word for it." He wrinkled his nose above the grey military moustache. "Look—I've got to get down to my car radio. To inform everybody that we've got this man. You two can, h'm, have a look in all that stuff meantime. Though I don't think you'll find anything, mind. But I'll send up a constable to give you a hand . . ."

"Oh, no—don't bother, sir. We'll manage all right," Ian said.

"There's a lot of this ghastly mud."

"Yes—but we only have to look where Dubitsky's tracks are. He couldn't have hidden anything anywhere else."

"No. That's true. Ah, well—I'll get along. And, er, good luck! Though I must say that, wherever the Countess of Borthwick's diamonds are, I can't imagine them in that bog! Don't be too long. A car will be waiting for you, down at the railway bridge."

Their friend turned and strode off. There are some things that are just not suitable for a superintendent of police to do.

The boys peeled off sandals and stockings, and stepped into the cold, black, slimy mud. Their feet sank in only an inch or two. It was a most peculiar sensation as the stuff came squelching up between their toes. Although it felt unsafe, as though they might sink in deeply, obviously that was nonsense when a man so much larger and heavier than themselves had been safe enough. They followed Dubitsky's tracks exactly. His right footprint was in each case deeper than the left; his limp would have caused that.

By his tracks the man had clearly made straight for the highest, or the deepest, group of peat mounds, approximately in the centre of the bog area. This was where the action of water and frost and wind had cut down into the heather and the soft peat soil beneath, to form a sort of cliff-and-valley system in miniature. Here, where the banks reached a height of over three feet, Dubitsky had crouched in hiding.

The footmarks showed that he had moved about a bit amongst these little cliffs—no doubt to find the best cover from view in all directions.

The boys began to search the heather that still grew on top of the larger banks; there would have been the easiest place to thrust in the jewels, out of sight. Although they practically uprooted and bared every top that the man's tracks showed to have been within his reach, however, they uncovered nothing more exciting than a number of very large and active beetles, and a deserted bird's nest. They were very careful about where they trod, themselves, so as not to trample out Dubitsky's tracks.

Unsuccessful in their first attempt, they began a systematic search of the peat-banks themselves. Fortunately, by its very nature, peat soil shows very clearly where it has been recently disturbed. And there were very few places where there was the least sign of any disturbance. None that they saw looked as though disturbance had been deliberate, either—just a tussock of heather pulled away, where the fugitive had probably dragged himself up, or a crumbling away of the bank where he had leant or rubbed against it. Although the brothers poked and probed about in these places very thoroughly indeed, there was nothing to be found, absolutely no indication of any attempt to hide anything.

"Could he have made a hole, somewhere, put the jewels in, and sort of plastered it over again with peat mud, I wonder?" Ian suggested.

"Not without it showing. The soil up on the higher parts of these hags is very different from the black mud below—much drier and browner and crumbly. It would show."

"Yes. I'm afraid so. But he must have hidden the diamonds somewhere . . ."

They turned their attention to the basic mud on which they walked—what is called peat-broth, sticky and black and objectionable. It seemed unlikely, surely, that anyone would actually push jewels and necklaces down into that, when they could be so much more satisfactorily hidden up in the heather or in the dry soil. Here, of course, the man's tracks were useful in showing the only places where he *could* have buried anything—but at the same time they could have covered up and trodden over any such spot. There was nothing for it but to dig down below every footprint.

This, a most unpleasant and laborious business, the twins did. They used their fingers for the job, for the mud was soft enough—and in almost less time than it takes to tell they were covered from head to foot in black slime. It was extraordinary how the peat-broth managed to spread itself over their persons. But dig and scoop and puddle as they would, their fingers met nothing more solid than bits of heather root and pieces of quartz gravel.

At last, wearily, hopelessly, they stood up—looking for all the world like a pair of badly-made-up darky minstrels.

"It's no use," Ian said flatly. "They're not here. The super was right. Whatever Dubitsky did with those jewels, he didn't hide them here—if he ever had them at all."

"Of course he had them!" Don exclaimed determinedly. "Don't be a defeatist!"

"I'm not. But . . . well, if he didn't have them on him just now, and he didn't leave them here—where are they?"

"Somewhere between here and Rulekirk Station," his brother said, frowning. "He had them then, I'm sure. He was running away with them—you *know* he was!"

Ian groaned aloud. "There's a lot of Scotland between here and Rulekirk Station!"

CHAPTER FOURTEEN

HIDE AND SEEK

THEY went downhill, side by side and very depressed, looking for a burn in which to wash themselves. The very peat soil with which the hill was covered, however, ensured that water seeped away through it rather than drained into streams. There were no burns here. The best thing they could find was a ditch running along the side of the railway cutting itself, in which some dark brown fluid lay, rather like oxtail soup. Bathing their faces and hands in this, somewhat doubtfully, at least had the effect of making them laugh at the spectacle each presented, and so helped to cheer them up slightly. They went off southwards along the line, their blackness much more evenly distributed and well rubbed in. Don described the assault in the train.

"Don," Ian interrupted presently, snatching up long grasses and docken leaves to wipe his hands dry on. "We've got to think about this. Really think it all out. I'm sure, if we put our minds to it, we'll think of something. You said back there, that the jewels are somewhere between here and Rulekirk Station. But that really only means between where the train stopped finally and that peat-hag. Don't you agree? Unless Dubitsky threw the jewels out of the train window—which doesn't seem likely."

"That's true, yes. Of course. It would be daft to think of him throwing them out. He did open the window once, I remember. But I'm pretty sure that he didn't throw anything out. It was when we stopped just after Riccarton Junction—no, not stopped. Just when we were going very slowly. I think he looked out, forward, to see what was delaying us . . ."

"Yes, yes," Ian said, a little impatiently. "I don't for a moment believe that he would throw out the swag anyway. He may have been a bit concerned about the train going so slowly, but I don't suppose that it would be until he saw the police cars actually racing the train that he would realise that there was anything seriously enough wrong to think of getting rid of the jewels. It stands to reason. But . . . once he decided that it was time that he did a bolt from the train, then, by the same reasoning he maybe felt that it might be time to get rid of the loot."

"Agreed. Go on."

"Well, then—since we decided that he would never leave the stuff in the train itself, hidden behind the seating or anything—the chances of him ever seeing it again would be nil—it seems ten to one that he hid it somewhere after he jumped down and started running. But apparently before he reached the peat-hag valley. You say that you kept him in sight all the time until he disappeared over the ridge, back there, into the hags?"

"Yes, that's right. I would have seen him bending down and hiding something, however quick he was about it."

"Unless he fell. Stumbled. It might not look as though he was hiding anything. If he did it deliberately."

"He couldn't really hide anything, that way. I mean, he wouldn't have time. Without it looking phoney. I wasn't so very far behind."

"Maybe not. But *did* he stumble at all? That you can remember? It just might be important."

Don furrowed his muddy brows, trying to recollect. "I don't think so. He was limping all the time, of course. He sort of tripped quite often. Especially when climbing up the hill. But I don't remember him actually going down, his hands touching the ground. I think I would have noticed that."

"He might just have *thrown* the jewels away somewhere, I suppose—but it would have to have been somewhere easily recognisable if he was ever going to find them again. A spot he could fix upon. Also, where you wouldn't notice them as you passed. Not very easy for him. I don't see anything like that along this length of track, do you?"

"Just a minute," Don said. "He did fall. Once. Now I come to think of it, he was down on his hands and knees when I looked down on him, that time, from the train. Just after he had jumped. Before I opened my own door and jumped down on to the line myself. Yes, he was."

"You mean, in jumping down he had fallen, and was picking himself up?"

"Well, that's what I thought. At least, I never really thought about it at all. I was feeling a bit groggy. But that's what seemed to have happened. It's quite a big jump. But . . . it has just occurred to me that if that's all it was, he ought not to have been so long about it. I mean, still bent down like that. He must have been down there quite a bit. I remember sitting on my seat for a while after he'd opened his door. Trying to get my breath back, and all that. Before I got up and looked. My head was going round . . ."

"By Jove—I think you were jolly brave. To go after him at all, after that! I don't think I'd have had the nerve to do it. If he had turned on you again, out in open country, it wouldn't have been very nice . . . !"

"I . . . I thought of that!" Don admitted, grinning a little sheepishly. "But . . . that's not what I'm trying to tell you. What I mean is that it all took a little while. After he must have jumped out. As I started to open the door—or at least to pull down the window so as I could get my hand out to open it—there he was, just getting up, and sort of grovelling about on the ground as he did so. So, either he had lain there, after jumping, for quite a while, or . . . or . . ."

"By Jove!" Ian cried. "Come on!" and he began to run.

They thudded along the path at the side of the line, Don only a yard or so behind his brother.

When they got back, panting now, to approximately where the train had been stopped, according to Don, they looked about them rather uncertainly.

"Here?" Ian asked. It was on a longish stretch of line, and there was nothing much to indicate where thereon the train had been standing. "Are you sure this is where it was?"

"Well . . . not exactly," his brother admitted. "It's a bit difficult. But it would be *about* here." He stared about him, at the bleak landscape, to see if there was anything there that he could remember having noticed, that would establish the position more precisely. But he had been much too busy looking at the police cars, at Dubitsky down on the line, and making up his own mind as to what to do, to be considering the landscape.

"There must be *some* way of placing the spot," Ian said. "Is there nothing that you can remember, Don?"

"Well . . . not that I can think of. I'm trying to think back. I wasn't looking for landmarks, you know."

"No. But . . . is there nothing about when you actually began to run? Along this cinder path? Nothing that strikes you as familiar?"

"No, I don't think so. Not specially. But—just a moment. When I first saw the cars. Up on the hillside. They were just like two black beetles. It's a good long way off, you know—the road. You can't actually see it, from here. To check up that it *was* the road, I looked back and saw the telegraph poles there, stretching away back northwards over the crest of that hill. You can see them there now." He pointed. "Well, thinking back, I can remember now that it was a moment or two before I recognised that they *were* telegraph poles. That was because the most obvious one on the skyline was so thick. Not like a pole, at all. Then I noticed others, much more slender, on either side. Mind you, they were all nearly two miles away up there. D'you see what I'm getting at? The thick one wasn't just one, at all. It was two or three of them, seen in line, one behind an other. So if we could find a spot, down here on the railway, where we could line up those poles the same way as they were before . . ."

"I say—that's jolly cute!" Ian said admiringly. "Like the way fishermen do with landmarks ashore, to let them know when they're over their fishing grounds?"

"That's what I mean, yes."

"Which way do you think we should move, to look? I mean, it's obviously not just here. All the poles can be seen individually from here."

"You go back a bit—and I'll go forward."

They paced away from each other, gazing, over opposite shoulders, up at the long brown heather slope to the north-west. It was Don who shouted, after a few moments, and Ian came running back.

"There it is," he exclaimed. "See? From here those three poles look like one very thick one. That's just as I remember it. It must have been just about here where I was standing. In my compartment."

They were both staring down at the cinder path at their feet, now. There were plenty of foot tracks thereon. It was very narrow—no more than a couple of feet from where the whitened stones in which the sleepers were bedded ended and the grass of the verge began. But there was nothing particularly significant about this section of path that they could see—and no sign of any marks or crushing of the longish grass behind.

"This *is* the side of the train that you jumped from?" Ian asked.

"Of course. We were facing the road, with the cars, all the time."

"Well, I suppose that these footprints will tell us something if we really try to read them properly."

There were the marks of many feet on that path, naturally, especially on the slightly muddy patches—made by the guard, the police, and themselves, as well as Dubitsky. Most of these were going in both directions. What they were looking for were deeper impressions, probably only of the toes of boots and sandals, and pointing outwards, not along the line, where the man and Don had jumped down. The guard would have got down too, from his van—but they reasoned that he, being used to it, would have climbed down less hurriedly and his tracks would be less obvious.

Not that there was anything obvious about those that they were looking for. Nothing of the sort indeed showed. The surface of the path was moist enough in the main to show prints up pretty clearly, and the boys had had ample opportunities to memorise Dubitsky's hobnailed-boot tracks up on the peat. The boys' own sandal marks of course were easily identified too, by their size and crepe soles.

Though other and larger footprints much obscured most of the tracks that they wanted to see, yet they could identify here and there both the hobnail boots and the sandals—but heading along the line both northwards and southwards, not facing outwards at all. What this meant occurred to them both simultaneously.

"Look," Ian said. "We can't be at the right place, after all. Some of these tracks are going upline and some down. The down ones must have been made by Dubitsky and the police as they brought him back here. All these ones with rubber soles must be the police. But Dubitsky's upline ones show here—so that must mean that he was already on the run when he made them. In other words that he jumped down from the train farther *down*line. We must be too far upline, despite your telegraph poles."

"M'mmm. That's true. Yet I could have sworn . . ."

"Maybe there is some other spot where the poles

run together in the same way? Another group of the poles, perhaps?"

"Must be, I suppose." Don sounded a little crestfallen. He had been rather proud of that piece of deduction from memory.

They moved off down the line again, slowly, taking care to walk on the grass so as not to further confuse the tracks on the path.

Sure enough, in perhaps another forty yards they found a spot where the poles up on the hillside merged again into a single thick pillar—presumably not exactly the same group of poles.

"This might happen time and again, I suppose," Don complained. "And I thought I'd struck a wonderful pointer. There doesn't seem to be any marks here, either. Just the same up and down footprints."

"Yes. But your idea is a help, just the same," Ian pointed out. "There may be quite a number of spots where the poles run together like that, with so many of them, and the hillside on such a slow open curve. But it does mean that the point we want is one of them. I mean, exactly. So it's just a question of checking on them all."

Don nodded. "I'm not so clever as I thought I was, though. Let's try again."

"Yes. I wish there hadn't been so much marching about. It's a blessing that there seems to be only the one pair of hobnailed boots. If the police had worn them, too, instead of these rubber-soles, we'd have been sunk."

Actually they came to another point where the line of poles could be seen to run together, in only another dozen yards or so. And here, quite plainly, they could see that there had been trampling on the grass verge beside the signal wires.

"This may be it," Ian cried. "Look—all that disturbance of the grass. For some reason somebody stepped off the path there . . ."

"Goodness—here's a policeman coming," Don warned. "He must have been sent back to see what we're up to. Here he comes clumping along with his great feet! We'll have to keep him off, somehow—or he'll trample everything . . ."

Ian was not listening. Suddenly he pounced forward, to point. "See—see where those big rubber soles have squelched to one side? Well, just beyond them—nearly into the grass. That is the toe-cap of Dubitsky's boot, I'm sure. Look—the mark is quite plain. Facing *inwards*, not outwards. See?"

"Yes. And here's the mark of the other boot. Not so clear. They're at right angles to all the other prints. But . . . they're facing towards the line. That's strange. I had been looking for them facing the other way."

"It's just the toe-caps. As though he'd jumped down. But he wouldn't jump *facing* the train, would he?"

"No. He couldn't, anyway. Not so close to the line

Ian was already crouching down.

as these marks show. In fact, now I come to think of it, I think that *I* landed on the grass when I jumped. He would, too. That's what all the crushing means."

"Then . . . this means that he'd turned round. These are only the tips of his boots. Toe-caps. So he must have been crouching down, on his haunches. Facing the train. Doing what?"

"You know—I do believe that he *was* facing the train. When I looked out and saw him down there. Yes, he was. Not facing the other way, as he should have been. I didn't think of it, at the time. He was scrabbling away at something, too . . ."

Ian was already crouching down in turn, presumably exactly in the place that Dubitsky had done so, facing the rails. Opposite him, directly across the little pathway was the butt-end of a wooden sleeper projecting from its bed of bleached stones. Underneath it there was a slight hollowing. And there, amongst the stones, and almost of the same pale colour, a corner of newspaper could just be seen.

"Don!" Ian exclaimed urgently, and reached over, his hand trembling a little, to push aside the loose stones. He drew out a roughly folded-up parcel made out of a page or two of newsprint. The paper parted somewhat, owing to the quivering of the excited boy's hand. From its crushed and crumpled folds the afternoon sun struck a positive blaze of dazzlement.

"Well, well—what goes on here?" a deep voice sounded, close by, and almost guiltily the brothers looked up. A constable, not one of those who had been active on the hill, stood above them. "What have you two got there?"

Ian began to open up the paper—and out on to the muddy footpath poured the most brilliant and scintillating cascade that it had ever been the boys' fortune to behold. Flashing and gleaming in the slanting sunlight were diamonds, rubies, emeralds, pearls, in strings and ropes, in brooches and rings and clasps. Left in the paper, in Ian's muddy hand, was the most splendidly sparkling of all, a great necklace of matched and mounted diamonds, large and small, that seemed to glow and glitter with its own cold fire.

Breathless, the brothers stared.

"Pick them up, then," the policeman ordered, indignantly. "Don't go dribbling these things on the ground, that way. Those trinkets are worth money, goodness me. Fancy you two stumbling on them like that! Here, give them to me. These things have got to be looked after."

Ian and Don were too full of emotion to protest, or even to speak, almost all the way back to the police car waiting for them by the railway bridge. They kept looking at each other, wonderingly, at a loss for words.

News of the discovery was radioed from the patrol car straight away, and the superintendent's Jaguar came roaring back over the hills to meet them before they were half-way back to Rulekirk. The jewels were handed over to him, and the boys transferred to his car.

"So-o-o!" The superintendent looked at the contents of the folded newspaper, and then to the boys. "Very nice. Very nice indeed. So you were right, eh? You beat me to it, after all! Tucked under a railway sleeper. Why didn't I think of that, now?"

"Well, we didn't actually think of it either, sir," Ian admitted honestly. "We just sort of got there, one thing leading to another, you know. It was the telegraph poles on the hill, the tracks, and the footprints that took us there in the end. Dubitsky's hobnailed boots. And Don remembering about seeing the line of poles."

"It's a good thing that the police wear rubber-soled boots," Don added. "If they'd worn studs or tackets, like Dubitsky, we'd never have found those jewels, I think."

"Well, that's something to think about!" the officer acknowledged, smiling. "Pretty good deduction on your part, just the same. You seem to have been right, more or less, all along the line. Much more right than I was . . ."

"Oh, well," Ian said, uncomfortably. "We were just lucky, really. And you *were* right about the jewels not being in the peat bog."

"So I was," the other acknowledged gravely. "To tell you the truth, I was not at all anxious to search that dirty black hole!"

"All the same, *we* were right about Dubitsky having them on him," Don, less soft-heartedly, pointed out. "Up till the time that he jumped out of the train."

"Yes, you were," the superintendent nodded. "I admit it. Absolutely right. In other ways, too. He *was* on his way—we managed to get that out of him, at last. To Liverpool. Then, probably, to South America. Set up for life—a rich man. Well, the court will set him up now—though not *quite* for life, I suppose! But for quite a while. Mr. Dubitsky ought to be kept out of trouble for quite some time. Thanks to you two entirely." The other smiled, genially now. "All I can say for the police is that we got you there! Got you there in time."

"You got the train stopped, too," Ian pointed out. "We couldn't have done that."

"No. I suppose that would have been a bit beyond even you two! Still, you'd have had a good try at it, I'll be bound! Legally or otherwise!"

The twins were uncertain whether to laugh or not.

"Och, well . . ." Don said. He was thinking about Mickey Pat.

"Well, thank you both, anyway. And, talking about thanks—I think I know somebody who's going to be very grateful indeed. Even more grateful than the police. To you two. For getting these bits and pieces back. This one especially." He birled the diamond necklace round and round on one finger, so that it seemed to send out sparks and flashes. "The Countess of Borthwick ought to bless your young hearts. She might even bestow on each of you a right honourable kiss!"

"My goodness—I hope she doesn't!" Don exploded. The brothers looked at each other, appalled.

CHAPTER FIFTEEN

MICKEY PAT'S FAREWELL

As the big car swept eastwards down Teviotdale, the two boys sitting together in the back seat grew more and more uncomfortable. The superintendent's broad back was turned to them, stiff, unrelenting, and most official-seeming. There was nothing that they could do but sit and wait.

Presently Don nudged Ian's arm, and nodded, forward. Away in front of them, high on a spur of the north side of the great dale, Houndswyre Tower had just come into view, straight and tall.

None the happier for sighting it, the twins sat silent.

The car left the main highway and began to climb up on to the rising ground to the north, by a road which would eventually bring them to Lilliesleaf and Melrose. This was not the route that the boys usually took to the Tower, since it would have given them a longer climb on their bicycles. It led actually along the summit of the lengthy hog's-back ridge at the end of which the tower stood, and which separated the valley of the Swale from that of Teviot.

They had less than a mile to go along here when suddenly Don again nudged his brother—but very differently from the previous occasion. This was an urgent dig. He was gazing out of the window, down to the left, down towards the Swale Water. A narrow side road wound its way along there, following the twists of the valley—the same road on which the Humber shooting-brake had come to grief, indeed, four nights before. A single figure was walking along there, westwards, small and lonely-seeming, the only moving thing visible. It was too far to distinguish features—but the walker had a most noticeable limp, and there was a sort of faint reddish halo about his head. Despite his limp, he seemed to be trudging most determinedly westwards.

The twins looked at each other, and their breaths came out in a long sigh of relief. They smiled, briefly but broadly, happily, and settled back in their seats. They said never a word.

Presently the big Jaguar came over the rise opposite Houndswyre Tower, and drew up where the brothers had been in the habit of leaving their bicycles. Somehow, the whole scene looked a little different now.

"Well—this is it," the superintendent said. "I don't think that we need hide this time." He got out, waiting for the boys. "This one won't run away very fast, from what you tell me, if he has a badly injured leg. Come along."

"Yes, sir," the brothers said in chorus, following on

through the gate. The superintendent did not bother to take his driver along as a reinforcement.

They slanted down across the grassy dip and up through the gorse bushes to Houndswyre Tower.

"Nice spot for a hide-out, right enough," the officer commented. "A bit draughty, though. Where did you say that your Irish friend roosts?"

"He *was* down in a sort of dungeon, sir. Under the stairway," Ian answered. "Down some steps. Less draughty there, I suppose. But . . . he may not be there now, of course."

"Why not? He's been there for four days, you say?"

"He might suddenly have felt better," Don suggested. "Well enough to move about a bit. You never know."

They went inside, the superintendent having to stoop to get through the doorway. Then they climbed down into the pit, the officer lighting the way with a pencil torch. The place was revealed as tidier than usual, tidier than the boys had ever seen it, in fact. The sacks had been emptied of their grass and bracken, and lay neatly folded. On top of them lay the bottles in which had been beer, milk and cold water. Then a cup and an enamel plate that they had brought the injured man. And, plainly to be seen, sandwiched between the cup and the plate, a pound note.

The twins said nothing.

"M'mmm," the superintendent observed, playing his

torch on all this. "It looks almost as though our bird has flown, after all. I wonder, now . . . ?"

"It does, rather, doesn't it," Don agreed.

"Quite gone," Ian declared. "Definitely. And for good, I'd say."

"Oh, yes. I think so, too. Look at that pound note. That will be his way of saying thank you. Quite decent of him, too."

"Yes. He's left everything very nice and tidy, I must say. Been quite busy, hasn't he."

"Gone to quite a lot of trouble . . ."

The superintendent cleared his throat loudly. "You two don't sound exactly broken-hearted about this. About this character's disappearing trick. Do you?" That was heavily said, almost an accusation.

"Er . . . well, no."

"Not really. I mean . . . well, no."

"In fact, I'd say that the pair of you are as pleased as Punch!"

"Oh. Well, you see, sir—we got rather fond of Mickey Pat, in a sort of way."

"He wasn't such a bad chap—once you got to know him. A bit moody, of course, but . . ."

"He was a law-breaker, wasn't he? He was a criminal. A common crook, in fact."

"Oh, I don't think he was, really. Do you, Don? Not really a crook," Ian protested. "I think that he was just sort of led astray, you know. By Dubitsky. They were mates together. On this concrete-mixer, you see.

I'm sure he wasn't like Dubitsky. He said, on his word of honour, that he hadn't stolen the jewels. We asked him . . ."

The superintendent's snort was eloquent.

"He really just drove the car for Dubitsky," Don pointed out.

"A stolen car. And he wrecked it. Anyway, he helped in committing two serious crimes. He could get a couple of years for that. And should, boy!"

"Oh, no! That would be awful . . ."

"He's suffered an awful lot, really, you know. Already," Ian pointed out urgently. "He's had terrible pain. Lying here in this black, damp hole for days. Deserted by his mate. And he won't be able to work for a good while because of his ankle. Surely all that is punishment enough?"

"The law wouldn't say so, laddie. The law doesn't do things in that soft-hearted, soft-headed way, you know. And just as well."

"No. But then . . ." Ian hesitated. "The law hasn't really done anything very much, as yet, has it? Hard-headed, or any other way." That came out in a rush. "It's . . . well, it's the soft-headed, soft-hearted ones who've done everything, so far. Isn't it, sir?"

The superintendent drew a hand over his mouth, perhaps to hide its expression. "I . . . h'mm . . . see what you mean, young man," he said gravely. "You may have something there, perhaps."

"You don't mind me saying so . . . ?"

"Not at all, not at all. An entirely just remark, I'm afraid." He looked around him, and then switched off the torch. "It rather looks as though it is going to be quite difficult to pursue this case against . . . er, what did you say his name was?"

"Mickey Pat, sir. We don't know his other name. His real name. He never told us."

"Dear me—is that so? Nameless, unknown, and disappeared! Pretty hopeless case, I'm afraid, isn't it? All we know about him, in fact, is that he's a rotten driver and has a bad leg, a limp. And after all, there are lots of people who limp, many of them bad drivers, I expect. So . . ."

"So . . . ?"

"So I think it's high time that you two got away home to your auntie's for your tea," the superintendent said. "Case closed."

"Oh! Really, sir? Thank you."

"That's jolly decent of you . . ."

"I could do with a cup myself, come to think of it. It's been quite an afternoon. Come along, softies!"

CHAPTER SIXTEEN

POSTMAN'S KNOCK

Two mornings later, the postman brought no fewer than three letters to Lilac Cottage, Denholm-on-the-Green. The boys' aunt was most pleasurably excited, for she was not in the habit of receiving a lot of mail—until she put on her glasses and discovered that they were all for her nephews.

The first, on a page torn from an exercise book, was in pencil, and in very rough and ill-formed writing, was addressed to "the macdonald Buoys, Lilack cotage, Denhome," and read:

"Dear Buoys,

this is just to thank you very much for being such a help I dont know what id done without you and I shall not go poching again or *anything else* like that thats a promiss ive lerned my lesson this time.

im going back to old ireland to my old Mother god bless her so will not be seeing you again i hope your anty keeps well.

thank you mickey pat."

The second, on official notepaper, was from the chief constable, the Border Counties Constabulary. It was typewritten, and said:

"Dear Ian and Don MacDonald,

I wish to say, on behalf of my colleagues and myself, how much we all appreciate and admire the good work you put in over the tracing and capture of the accused Stefan Dubitsky, and the recovery of the missing jewels from Swaleholm House. Without your quick wits, courage and great determination, this man undoubtedly would still be at liberty, and the stolen property perhaps lost to its owner for ever.

Superintendent Murray has told me all about your exploits, and I intend to give myself the pleasure of meeting you both shortly. I hope that if there is ever anything that the Border Counties Constabulary can do for you in return, you will not hesitate to apply to,

Yours sincerely,

Thomas Duncan,

Chief Constable."

And the third letter, written on very heavy and elegant notepaper indeed, slightly scented, with a coronet embossed on both paper and envelope, was addressed from Swaleholm House.

"My dear young Friends and Benefactors,

I cannot tell you how grateful I am to you both for getting me back my precious jewellery, my wonderful necklace especially, a famous heirloom in this family. It is quite impossible for me to put down in words all I feel about your splendid actions. However, as I understand that you are at present on holiday with your aunt in Denholm, perhaps you would care to come here and tell me all about it one day soon? Do let me know when, and I shall send my car for you.

Meantime, please each try to think of something that you may have wanted very much indeed but never really hoped to get. Something exciting—like a motor-scooter (perhaps you are too young for this?) or a cine-camera and projector, or even a sailing dinghy. Something like that, which it will give myself and my husband the greatest of pleasure to present to you. You can tell us what you've decided upon when you come. Remember, the cost is no object.

For the present, deep and sincere gratitude and good wishes.

Sincerely,

Judith Borthwick."

"By Jove!" Don, finishing first, burst out. "By Golly! Oh, I say!"

Ian swallowed, and moistened his lips. "Goodness!" he managed to get out. "A . . . a sailing dinghy! My hat—even if she does insist on kissing us, it'll be worth it!"

THE END